Gregg Press
Mystery Fiction Series

Otto Penzler, *Editor*

THE MAN
WITH THE
GETAWAY FACE

THE MAN WITH THE WITH THE GETAWAY FACE

RICHARD STARK

With a new introduction by
JUSTIN SCOTT

GREGG PRESS
A DIVISION OF G.K. HALL & CO., BOSTON, 1981

With the exception of the Introduction, this is a complete photographic reprint of a work first published in New York by Pocket Books in 1963.

The trim size of the original paperback edition was 4¼ by 6¼ inches.

Frontmatter design by Norman Quesnel.

Printed on permanent/durable acid-free paper and bound in the United States of America.

Republished in 1981 by Gregg Press, A Division of G.K. Hall & Co., 70 Lincoln St., Boston, Massachusetts 02111.

First Printing, May, 1981

Library of Congress Cataloging in Publication Data

Westlake, Donald E
The man with the getaway face.

(Gregg Press mystery fiction series)
Reprint of the ed. published by Pocket Books, New York.
I. Title.   II. Series.
PS3573.E9M3   1981   813.'54   80-29359
ISBN 0-8398-2707-5

INTRODUCTION

My friend and occasional mentor, Donald E. Westlake, is an innovator. Thus far in his career he has created not one, but *two* types of modern mystery-suspense novels and unless someone steals his typewriter, he'll probably invent a third. As a hundred imitators can tell you, Mr. Westlake is the creator and funniest practitioner of the comic-mystery wherein an appealingly buffoonish, thoroughly unassuming hero shambles through a plot that would make an ordinary man's teeth fall out, and emerges holding the hand of the attractive woman who got him into trouble in the first place. (Dortmunder fans will quibble about May's appearance, but she does bring home groceries and must be, if you stop and think about it, a beautifully romantic creature to cherish qualities in Dortmunder that a literal-minded observer might overlook.)

Parker novels are Westlake's second modern type. Writing as Richard Stark, he gave us a new kind of hero—a strong, taciturn and singleminded villain. But a thousand imitators can tell you that's not as easy as it sounds because Parker is not an anti-hero. There is nothing *anti* about Parker. He knows what he wants and goes out and gets it. Secondly, the other characters in the Parker novels have desires, shortcomings, and sometimes a heroism of their own. But where the reader sees vividly drawn, interesting human beings, Parker sees obstructions.

His whole world is peopled by obstructions, which is logical since making a living stealing things does go against the grain. That doesn't mean you don't like Parker. In fact you like him a lot because he does exactly what has to be done, and only what has to be done, and if he can't figure out what to do, he thinks about it.

The proof is that unlike the Exacerbator-Demol-
isher-Obliterator-crowd, Parker does not kill automatically. He
kills, to be sure—often so suddenly that you feel you've been
shot—but he kills when nothing else is practical.

The Man with the Getaway Face (1963) is the second novel of
the ongoing Parker series and we readers are treated to an early
look at the bones and blood that go into making a unique character
grow. Stark and Parker are still getting used to each other and
every now and then Parker says something that delights an old
fan.

An amateur insists that they need five men to heist an armored
car and Parker deadpans, "You want to lay a seige and starve them
out?" Other times he turns almost garrulous, where in a later
book we know he'll think the same thing while smoking cigarettes
for many hours in a dark room. Parker's being born and we're
there to watch.

And therein lies another surprise. He's been around a long
time. In the first novel, *The Hunter* (1962), we meet Parker
striding across the George Washington Bridge. But in *The Man
with the Getaway Face,* those of Richard Stark's friends and readers
who haven't noticed how low their canines are dragging, will be
amazed to discover that plot elements hinge upon the fact that the
Verrazano-Narrows Bridge hadn't been built when the novel was
written and that the only way off the New York side of Staten
Island was by ferryboat.

The best marvel, however, is that while Parker matured rapidly,
he never got stale. Vivid detail infected the novels from the start.
The outcast's sense of living in rented rooms and driving
borrowed trucks and other people's cars was strong from the
beginning, as were Stark's favorite themes—the clash of hope and
doubt, fear and greed, and the practicality of honor among thieves
and by extension the rest of us. Parker remains a good heist man
because he works hard and keeps his word. He remains interesting
because Richard Stark does the same.

Justin Scott
New York City

ONE

◆◆◆◆◆◆◆◆◆◆◆◆

I.

WHEN the bandages came off, Parker looked in the mirror at a stranger. He nodded to the stranger and looked beyond at the reflection of Dr. Adler.

Parker had been at the sanitarium a little over four weeks now. He had come in with a face that the New York syndicate wanted to put a bullet in, and now he was going back out with a face that meant nothing to anyone. The face had cost him nearly eighteen thousand, leaving him about nine from his last job to tide him over till he got rolling again. The syndicate trouble had been a bad time, but that was over now.

Parker stood a while longer at the mirror, studying the stranger. He had a long narrow nose, flat cheeks, a wide lipless mouth, a jutting jaw. There were tiny bunchings of flesh beneath the brows, forcing them out just a bit from the forehead, subtly changing the contours of the face. Only the eyes were familiar, flawed onyx, cold and hard.

It was a good job. Paid for in advance, it should be.

1

Parker nodded again at his new face, turned away from the mirror, and watched the doctor drop the bandaging into a wastebasket. "When can I get out of here?"

"Any time you're ready."

Dr. Adler was tall and bony and gray-haired. From 1931 till 1939 he had worked with the California Communist Party, setting up strike camps. After the Second World War, in which he had done plastic surgery in an Army hospital in Oregon, he had set up private practice in San Francisco. But in 1949 a Congressional Committee had exploded his past in his face. He wasn't stripped of his license, just of his livelihood. Since 1951 he had made his living as a plastic surgeon to those outside the law, operating a sanitarium front near Lincoln, Nebraska.

Dr. Adler crossed the room again, going to the door, where he paused. "When you're dressed, come down to the office. I have a letter for you."

"From Joe Sheer?"

"I think so."

Joe Sheer was the retired jugger who'd vouched for him with the doctor. When the doctor left, Parker opened the closet door and took out the new suit, a dark brown he'd bought on the way here and never worn. He chucked out of the white pajamas and into his clothes, and took one last look at himself in the full-length mirror on the back of the closet door. He was a big man, flat and squared-off, with boxy shoulders and a narrow waist. He had big hands, corrugated with veins, and long hard arms. He looked like a man who'd made money, but who'd made it without sitting behind a desk.

The new face went with the rest of him as well as the old one had. Satisfied, he picked up his suitcase and left the room and went downstairs to the office. The sanitarium was one large building, office and waiting room and staff living quarters on the first floor, patients' rooms on the second. There was space for twenty-three patients, and

Dr. Adler maintained a staff of four—two nurses, a cook, and a handy man. There was rarely more than one patient in the place and half the time there were no patients at all. But he had state licenses to worry about, and Federal taxes, so a large part of his take went for false front.

Parker went into the doctor's office. "I left some old clothes upstairs. You can throw them away for me."

"All right. Here." He held out an envelope.

Parker took it and ripped it open. Inside was a brief pencil-scrawled note:

Mr. Anson,

I understand you might be interested in a fast-moving investment with triple level protection, guaranteed to turn over a profit of at least fifty thousand in an incredibly short length of time. The stock is automotive, of course, and I understand its course has been carefully plotted against future profits. If you are interested, get in touch with Mr. Lasker in Cincinnati at your earliest convenience. He's at the Warwick.

JOE

Parker read the letter, then turned the envelope over and studied the flap. Dr. Adler said, "Yes, I steamed it open."

"You did a bad job," Parker told him. He dropped letter and envelope on the desk.

The doctor shrugged. "I get bored sometimes," he said. "So I read other people's mail."

"Joe said I could trust you."

"With your face. Not with your mail." He smiled, thinly. "I am a doctor, Mr. Anson. That is all I want to be. If circumstances had been different, I'd be a doctor in San Francisco today with more reputable patients and a more lucrative practice. It doesn't matter, I'm still a doctor. And that's all. A doctor, not an informer, not a thief. I've taken all the money from you I intend to take, and once you leave here we will undoubtedly never have dealings again. Unless you recommend someone else, of course, or need yet another face. I read that letter on a whim."

"You get whims often?"

"I never get whims that would cut off my supply of patients, Mr. Anson."

Parker considered, studying him. Joe had said he was a little off, but that it was nothing to worry about. Parker shrugged. "All right. Do you know what the letter meant?"

"I have no idea. I'd be fascinated to know, however."

"It's an armored car holdup. Three guards. The job is figured to make the grab while it's on a highway, instead of in a city. Fifty grand is what they figure my share would be." Parker reached down and flipped the letter closer to the doctor. "You see it there?"

The doctor read the letter, slowly, holding it in both hands. His hands were so clean they looked bleached. He nodded. "Yes, I see."

"Can your man give me a ride to town?"

"Of course. You'll probably find him in the kitchen."

"Thanks. I'll take my case."

"Oh, yes. I forgot." The doctor stood up, went over to the dark green safe in the corner and twisted the combination. He opened the door and took out a light brown typewriter case. The typewriter case contained eight thousand five hundred dollars, all of Parker's cash.

Parker took the case and picked up the suitcase. "I'll be seeing you around."

"I doubt it."

When Parker left, the doctor was studying the letter again, a thin smile on his lips.

2.

DR. ADLER'S handy man was punch-drunk, though he'd never been in the ring. He'd been a Party organizer in the thirties, among the migrant crop harvesters, and scab-wielded two-by-fours had scrambled his brains. His former fluency with dialectic was gone; these days the driving of a hydromatic Chrysler was the most complicated exercise his brain could handle. He was fifty-four and his face was lumpy, with scar tissue around the eyes. The doctor call him "Stubbs."

Parker found him in the kitchen, a stainless-steel room kept spotless because most of its equipment was never used. Stubbs sat on a steel table against one wall, holding a white coffee mug in both hands. The cook, a thin ex-whore named May, was reading the back of a box of Fab.

Parker said to Stubbs, "You're supposed to drive me into Lincoln."

Stubbs frowned at him. "We got a Chrysler."

"Am I being kidded, friend?"

"No," May said. To Stubbs, she said, "To the city, Stubbs. He wants you to drive him to the city." She turned back to Parker. "Did the doctor say it's okay?"

"Yeah."

Stubbs got down from the table, laboriously. "I never drove a Lincoln," he said "I drove a Rolls once. It belonged to a sympathizer. That was down south someplace, near Dago. They killed a Joe Goss that time, blew the whole thing wide open. It would of been a good strike up to then, a deputy drove over this little girl, broke her leg. But then—the guys had to kill that Joe Goss, and it was all

5

over." He scratched his cheek. The flesh was soft, and gave like dough under his fingernails. "Where you want to go?"

May answered him. "Down into town, Stubbs. The freight yards, I guess."

"You betcha."

Stubbs led the way through the garbage room and out the back door. The sanitarium property, wooded, climbed up a slope back of the building. The garage was a separate brick structure to the left of the main building, with a cock weather vane atop the peaked roof. There was room for four cars, but aside from the Chrysler there was only one other vehicle, a Volkswagen Micro-Bus.

Parker stowed his suitcase and typewriter case on the back seat of the Chrysler and climbed in front next to Stubbs. Stubbs backed out, left the car long enough to pull down the garage door, and then maneuvered in a wide U-turn and around the building and down the black-top road to the three-lane concrete highway to the city.

They rode in silence, Parker smoking and watching the scenery. The new face was beginning to feel strange. His forehead and cheeks were tight, as though glue had dried on them.

Before they reached the city, Stubbs pulled over to the shoulder of the road and stopped. He carefully shifted to neutral and put on the emergency brake, and then turned to Parker. His face was creased in concentration, as though he was having a hard time remembering the words. "I want to talk to you," he said. "I talk to all the patients, when they're ready to go."

Parker flipped his cigarette out the window, and waited.

"One time," said Stubbs, "there was a guy came here to get a new face. Doc gave it to him, and then he figured the best thing was to kill Doc, because then nobody'd know who it was under the new face. He didn't have to do that, because the Doc is one man you can trust with your life. But this guy wouldn't take that, so I had to take the new face away from him again. You follow me?"

Parker smiled at him. "You think you could take this face away from me?"

"No trouble at all," said Stubbs. "Don't come back, mister."

Parker studied him, but challenges were for punks. He shrugged. "A fella named Joe Sheer told me the doctor was straight. It's his word I take."

Stubbs' belligerence faded. "I just wanted you to know."

"Sure," Parker said.

They rode the rest of the way in silence. Stubbs let him off at the railroad station, and Parker bought a ticket for Cincinnati. He had a three-hour wait, so he checked his luggage and went to a movie.

3.

THE man calling himself Lasker was sitting on the edge of the bed when Parker came into the room. The Warwick was a fourth-rate Transient & Permanent hotel with a dirty stone face and no marquee, and Lasker's room was what Parker had expected, complete with green paint on plaster walls and a faded imitation Persian on the floor. The wood of the window frame was spreading along the grain, looking like eroded farmland.

The man calling himself Lasker, but whose name was really Skimm, looked up as Parker came into the room. He dropped the pint and reached under the pillow. Parker said, "Didn't Joe tell you about the new face?"

Skimm paused with the Colt Woodsman half out from under the pillow. He squinted and said, "Parker?"

"That's right."

Skimm held onto the Woodsman. "What name'd you use in Nebraska?"

"Anson."

Skimm nodded and shoved the Woodsman back under the pillow. "They did a good job on you," he said. "You made me drop my whisky."

Parker went over to the window and looked out—at brick building backs and rusted black metal constructions on roofs. Down below he could see a trapezoidal concrete-covered yard, scattered with garbage cans and bits of paper. "You picked a bad neighborhood, Skimm," he said.

Skimm was picking up the pint. Some had spilled, soaking into the carpet. He looked over at Parker and shrugged in embarrassment. "We haven't been bankrolled yet." He held the pint up and squinted at the inch of whisky left in the bottom of it. "I need this job," he said. "I admit it."

Parker knew about that. Skimm, like most men on the bum, lived from job to job; he spent more in one year than most make in five and was always broke, dressing and looking like a bum. How he did it, where it all went, Parker didn't know.

He worked it differently, spending the money and time between jobs living at the best resort hotels and dressing himself in the best clothes. There was no overlap between people he knew on and off the job. He owned a couple of parking lots and gas stations around the country to satisfy the curiosity of the Internal Revenue beagles, but never went near them. He let the managers siphon off the profits in return for not asking him to take an active part in the business.

He came back from the window. The room sported a

green leather chair, the rip across the seat patched with masking tape. Parker settled into the chair gingerly.

"All right. Who else is in it?"

"So far, only me and Handy McKay. I've got the earie out for Lew Matson and Little Bob Foley. Maybe we'll need more; it's all how we set it up."

"You want me to angle for the bankroll, huh?"

"You got the connections, Parker," Skimm said. He had watery eyes, of a pale blue. They looked at Parker when Parker was talking, but when Skimm was talking they looked everywhere else—up at the ceiling and over at the window and down at the near-empty pint and over at the pillow and then the other way at the door with the hotel regulations pasted on the back.

"I've got the connections," Parker agreed. "Who's the bird dog on this one?"

"It's a frill." Skimm looked embarrassed. "She's a busher," he said, "but she's okay."

"If she never worked this route before," Parker said, "where'd she get the connections?"

"Through me. I met her one time." Skimm now looked more embarrassed than before. He was a thin stub end of a man, all bones and skin with no meat. His head was long and thin, set on a chicken neck with knotty Adam's apple, and his face was all nose and cheekbones. The watery eyes were set deep in the skull, the jaw small and hard. "We get along," he said, "her and me." He said it apologetically, as though he knew an off-the-wall like him shouldn't be getting along with any woman. "She works in a diner. In Jersey."

Parker dragged his Luckies out of his pocket, shook one out and lit it. "I don't know," he said.

"She's straight, Parker. I been in this business long enough."

"I don't like it."

"I heard about what happened with your woman. That was a tough bit."

Parker shrugged. "She got in a bind, that's all. So now she's dead."

"Alma is okay, believe me."

"It isn't she's a woman," Parker said. "It's she's new, that's what I don't like. When a new fish does the fingering, most of the time the job goes sour."

"Sure," said Skimm. "I know that. Because they want their piece of the pie, but they got to be covered because they're known. But this time it's different. Alma's going to take off with me after it's over."

"We'll see. What's the setup?"

"Hold on, I'll show you." Skimm tilted the pint, emptied it, and set it on the night table. Then he went over to the dresser, opened the bottom drawer, and took out a manila envelope. There wasn't any table or writing desk in the room, so he went back and spread things out on the bed. Parker stood beside the bed and watched.

The first thing Skimm took out of the envelope was an Esso roadmap of New Jersey. "Here it is," he said. He opened the map and pointed a finger to the right hand side of it, near New York. "Here's where it is here, where it says Perth Amboy. See it? Route 9 comes south here, see, and down here a couple miles below Perth Amboy it splits. See? 9 keeps on south, and 35 heads off to the east and follows the shore."

Parker nodded. He could have seen it better if Skimm had kept his fingers out of the way, but he didn't say anything. He wasn't in any hurry, and every man has his own rate and style of telling a story. Try to hurry Skimm or make him talk without covering the map with his fingers and he'd just get confused.

"Okay," Skimm was saying. "Now, two miles farther south, 34 takes off. To the east again, same as 35. Right there, see it?"

"I see it."

"Okay. Now, about midway between those turnoffs there's the Shore Points Diner, on the west side of the road. Right in there, see? Between where those two red lines go off to the right."

"I've got it, Skimm. And that's where this Alma's a waitress."

"Right! Now, down here—" His fingers moved southward down the map. "Here's Freehold, down here, where 9 crosses 33. Now, there's the Dairyman's Trust, this bank, see, it's up here in Elizabeth, and they got a branch in Newark, and they got a branch down here in Freehold, too. Now, every other Monday there's this Wells Fargo armored car comes down from the main branch in Elizabeth down to Freehold, see? Down along route 9, here."

"And they stop at this Shore Points Diner," Parker said.

"That's it! This Freehold, it ain't much of a town, but the Dairyman's Trust is the biggest bank, I mean with branches in Newark and Elizabeth and all, so most of the business accounts all around Freehold are in that bank, see? So when the armored car comes down every other Monday, it carries enough dough to pay off two weeks of payrolls around Freehold, and any other dough the bank needs down there. We figure maybe fifty G, maybe more."

Parker frowned. "That's all? The way I read the letter, fifty thousand figured to be my split."

Skimm looked up, worried and apologetic and embarrassed. "Oh, no, Parker! I never told Joe nothing like that."

"Okay, I read it wrong, that's all."

"I mean, fifty G is the minimum figure, you see? It might be seventy, eighty, who knows?"

Parker dragged on his cigarette, flicking ashes onto the whisky stain on the carpet. "That means if I'm lucky I clear ten. Maybe only eight." He shook his head. "It isn't worth it."

Skimm's eyes flicked toward the empty pint, then looked back at the map. "It's an easy haul," he said wistfully. "If there was something better on the fire, I'd think that way, too. But I got no other jobs building, and I need the dough." He looked up at Parker, his mouth opened because of the lifted angle of his head. "You know of anything else?"

"No." That was the trouble. He had nothing else on the fire either, and he only had the nine grand. He couldn't pick and choose and plan, the way he'd want to. He had to build a stake, he had to have a money cushion.

"I'd like to have you in it, Parker," Skimm was saying, wistful again. "I know your work."

"Maybe it doesn't really need five men," Parker said thoughtfully. "That's a big crowd for an armored car heist. What's the play?"

"Yeah." Skimm reached for the envelope. "We figured to do it at the diner," he said. "Here, let me show you." He was all activity again, talking in a rush, as though he were afraid Parker would walk out on him before he was done. He pulled more paper out of the manila envelope, and found the sheet he wanted. "Here, here it is. See, this is the diner here, and the highway, and the parking lot."

Parker looked in among the pointing fingers. On the sheet of paper was a rough pencil drawing of the diner area, as seen from above. The diner was set back off the highway about six yards, with parking lots on both sides and at the rear. Across the front, between diner and roadway, was a patch marked 'Grass.' There was an X scrawled on one of the parking lots at the side, up close against the side of the building.

"Now they come in," said Skimm, pointing all over the sheet of paper, "every other Monday morning between ten-thirty and eleven. They never miss. There's the driver, and a guard sitting up in front with him, and the other guard in back. They've all been on this route for years, see? And they've got a pattern, they never change. They come in between ten-thirty and eleven, and they park right there where the X is." He tapped the X with his finger and looked up at Parker. "See it there?"

"I see it."

"Right," said Skimm. He looked down at the drawing again. "Then, the driver and the guard from in back go into the diner and have coffee and danish and take a leak, see, and then they go back to the car and the other guard comes in. Then when he's done they take off again. Maybe fifteen minutes for the whole thing."

Parker nodded.

Skimm took a deep breath. "Now," he said, "here's the way we figured it. We need two tractor-trailers, big ones. They trail the armored car down 9, see, hanging back a little so when they get to the diner the first two guys are already inside. They pull in and they park on each side of the armored car, see, they bracket it like, so you can't look into the armored car from either side. Alma works it in the diner so that side is closed to be mopped, see, so there won't be any customers close enough to the windows on that side to be able to see what's going on. And the trailers stick back far enough so you'd have to be right behind the armored car to tumble to anything, you see what I mean? But nobody will anyway because right after the trailers come in our car parks right behind the trailers, facing across them, you see the way it works? Here, I'll show you." Unnecessarily, he drew a U-shape, and explained.

Parker waited through it, nodding, beginning to lose his patience. He didn't like the job with an amateur doing the fingering and five guys cutting up a fifty thousand dollar pie after the finger's ten per cent and the bankroller's two-for-one were already taken out, and with the job already requiring two tractor-trailers and a car. And Skimm didn't even have them into the armored car yet.

Skimm finished his explanation and said, "Now, we've got two guys in the head, inside the diner. The driver and the guard always take a leak when they stop off there, it never misses, they're regular as clockwork. So they go in, and the two guys in there tap them and stow them away in a stall, see? And outside we got the other three, from the trucks and the car. They pump tear gas into the air vent on top of the cab—you know what that looks like? They got this thing on top—"

"I know what it looks like," Parker said.

"Okay." Skimm hurried even faster, sensing Parker's impatience. "That forces the guy out, see? We take the keys off him, tap him, transfer the dough to the car, and we all take off. The one truck goes up 9 here, see? North, up to South Amboy, it's maybe a mile, and cuts back south on 535, this little blue road here. The other truck goes south to 516, that's maybe four miles, and then cuts east. And the car, with the dough, takes this old dirt road —it isn't on this map, it goes from behind the diner across here to this unmarked road, this little one here—and south on the unmarked road to Old Bridge. We all come to-gether at Old Bridge, see, and back off east of the town there's this falling-down old farm. We meet there. We split up the boodle and take off. And see, the thing is, we get vehicles going off in three directions, so they don't know which way to look for us."

He looked up at Parker, hopeful and expectant. "What do you think?"

Parker shook his head and crossed the room to toss his cigarette out the window. When he turned back, he said, "You ever work an armored car job before, Skimm?"

Skimm's lips twitched. "No, I never did."

"That's what I figured. They got two-way radios, boy. You drop tear gas in there, right away he calls. Before he has to take a deep breath, there's state police all over us."

Skimm looked down at the map and papers, as though they'd betrayed him. "I didn't know that."

"And you don't make a getaway in a semitrailer," Parker went on. "They'd catch you before you reached fourth gear."

"Jesus, Parker—"

"Who worked up this scheme? Alma?"

"Most of it was her idea, yeah."

"Sure. She spent a lot of time leaning on the counter looking out there at that tin box wishing she could get her hands on the green inside and working it all out in her head, not knowing a thing about heisting or armored cars or anything else except how to draw a lousy cup of coffee."

"Aw, now, Parker—"

"I need cash," Parker said. "I'm in the job, on one condition."

"Name it."

"We throw that plan away and start from scratch. She gave us the setup, and it's a good one. Bracketing the wagon with trucks is good, too. From there on, we got to work something out from the beginning."

Skimm twitched all over trying not to show his relief. He'd never worked an armored car before, and he hadn't been sure of himself. He'd probably talked himself into a bind with the woman Alma, loud-talking about what an artist he was so he couldn't admit to her he didn't know whether her ideas were any good or not. He'd wanted Parker because he wanted somebody else to take over the operation.

Parker lit a new cigarette. "We'll do it with three men, not five. The pie's too small for five. You and Handy and me, and we split it three ways even. You and Alma can share your third between you any way you want."

"What about her ten per cent?"

"Give it to her out of your third. What the hell, she's traveling with you."

"Jesus, I don't know, Parker. I'd have to check with Alma on that."

"You two figured to take a third anyway, didn't you? And leave the other two-thirds for a four-man split. So what's the difference? You get the same dough as before, but with a cleaner, safer job."

"I guess so," Skimm said doubtfully. "I'd have to check with Alma."

"Check with the finger? Skimm, give me an answer now or the deal's off."

Skimm worried it over, staring anxiously at the empty pint. Finally, he said, "Okay, Parker. Three ways, even."

"All right. Let me see that map." Parker came over and took it from the bed. "Newark," he said. "There's a bar named the Green Rose. It's on Division Street. I'll meet you there next Monday night, ten o'clock."

"Okay, sure." Skimm got up from the bed, his lips twitching again. Parker knew he was anxious to go buy another pint. "Okay, Parker, I'm glad to have you in, I really am. I'll send word to Lew and Little Bob to forget it."

"Good."

"What you going to do now?"

"See about bankrolling. I know a couple of people in Baltimore. I'll figure three grand to cover it."

"Okay, fine. Listen, you want Handy with me? At the bar I mean."

"Sure."

"I'm glad to have you in, Parker."

"The Green Rose," Parker reminded him. "Next Monday, ten o'clock."

4.

ACROSS the river from Cincinnati, Ohio is Newport, Kentucky. Parker took the bus over and walked to Whore Row. Cincinnati is a clean town, so the Cincinnati citizens in search of action go across the river to Newport, which is a dirty town. Parker wandered around, walking up and down the streets, looking. It was eleven-thirty at night when he got to Newport, and nearly two in the morning before he found what he was looking for.

Ahead of him, a weaving drunk fumbled with his carkeys, trying to get into a car with Ohio plates. The car was a Ford, cream-colored, two years old. Except for Parker and the drunk the block was empty and deserted.

Parker came along, arms swinging loose at his sides, and when he was alongside the drunk he turned and chopped him in the kidney. That made it impossible for the drunk to cry out. Parker turned him and clipped him, and caught the car keys as they fell from the drunk's hand. The drunk hit the pavement, and Parker unlocked the car door, slid behind the wheel, and drove away.

He took the bridge back across the river to Cincinnati and parked near the railroad depot. He went into the depot and got the suitcase and typewriter case from the locker where he'd stashed them. Then he went back to the car and drove north through town and out the other side and headed northeast on 22 toward Pittsburgh. It was now three o'clock Thursday morning. He had till Monday night to get to New Jersey and look the situation over for himself. If the setup looked as promising as Skimm had

17

made it sound, fine. Otherwise, Skimm would have a long
wait at the Green Rose.

Parker covered the three hundred miles between Cincinnati and Pittsburgh in under seven hours, crossing into
Pennsylvania at Weirton a little after nine. He circled
Pittsburgh, not wanting to go through town, and when he
got back to 22 on the other side it was after ten. He slowed
down, then, looking for a motel.

When he found one, he stopped. He slept most of the
day, getting up at quarter to seven. He took a shower and
shaved and dressed, and then opened the typewriter case
on the bed. He counted out three thousand dollars, then
closed the typewriter case again. He needed money badly,
so he'd decided to bankroll the job himself. So far as
Skimm was concerned, the money was coming from the
contacts in Baltimore.

Parker stowed the three thousand in his suitcase, then
carried the typewriter case down the row of doors to the
motel office. This was a secondary route now that the
Pennsylvania Turnpike was in existence, and the motel
was seedy and run-down. The interior walls needed a new
coat of paint, and half the neon sign out by the road wasn't
working.

The man who ran the motel was short, fat and balding.
His eyes shone behind glasses with plastic frames
patched by friction tape. He sat at the counter in the motel
office, dressed in a rumpled suit and a frayed white shirt
and a wrinkled tie. He had sullen lines around his mouth,
and he was surly whenever his customers spoke to him.

He was alone at the desk when Parker came in, staring
glumly across the counter through the plate-glass window
at the road. A semi passed, headed east, and then the road
was empty again.

Parker put the typewriter case up on the counter and
said, "Want to make half a G?"

The owner looked at him. "Why don't you go to hell?"

Parker lit a cigarette and dropped the match on the counter, still burning. The owner made a startled sound and reached out, slapping the match. Parker said, "One of these days, somebody's going to break your head."

"You get the hell out of here!" the owner said angrily. "Who do you think you are?"

"Five hundred," Parker said. "You could get the sign fixed."

The owner got off his stool, looking back at the phone on the wall. Then he looked at Parker again. "You mean it?"

Parker waited, smoking.

The owner considered, gnawing on the inside of his cheek. He stood next to his stool, one hand flat palm down on the counter. His fingernails were ragged and dirty. He thought about it, gnawing his cheek, and then he shook his head. "You're talking about something illegal," he said. "I don't want no part of it."

Parker opened the typewriter case. "See? Five grand. And it isn't hot money. I want to stash it someplace where I know it's safe. If I ask you to hold it for me and you look in it and see the dough, you might be tempted. So I pay you five hundred. You've made a nice piece of change, and you don't get so tempted."

"Five thousand." He said it with a kind of heavy contempt. "What would I do with five thousand? Where would I go? What would it get me? I'd need a lot more than that. I'm stuck in this rattrap for the rest of my life."

"You want the five hundred?"

"If a state trooper comes in looking for that money, I'll hand it right over. I don't go to jail for no five hundred dollars. Or any five thousand, either."

"I told you, it isn't hot."

The owner looked at the money. "For how long?" he asked.

Parker shrugged. "Maybe a week, maybe a year."

"What if it gets stolen off me?"

Parker smiled thinly, and shook his head. "I wouldn't believe it," he said.

"I don't know." The man looked at the money doubtfully. "Why don't you put it in a bank?"

"I don't like banks."

The owner sighed and nodded. "All right," he said. "I'll get the sign fixed."

Parker reached into the typewriter case and counted five hundred dollars onto the counter. Then he closed and locked the typewriter case and slid it across to the owner. "I'll stop back for it sometime," he said.

Then he went back to the room and picked up the suitcase. He stashed it in the Ford and left the motel, heading east.

It was after midnight when he reached New Jersey. He stayed north of Philadelphia and crossed the Delaware River from Easton to Phillipsburg, still on 22. He stayed with 22 all the way to Newark. When he reached Newark, he drove around the sidestreets for a while, and made two stops.

The first time, he took a screwdriver and removed the Jersey plates from a five-year-old Dodge. The second time, he took a razor blade from his shaving kit, and walked three blocks until he found an unlocked parked car. The street was deserted, so he slid behind the wheel and spent three minutes with the razor blade carefully removing the state inspection sticker from the windshield. It tore in a couple of places, but not badly. He went back to the Ford, found route 9, and drove south out of Newark.

About twenty miles south, he passed the Shore Points Diner, all lit up, with three trucks and a station wagon parked at the sides. He continued south, nearly to Freehold, and when the highway narrowed to two lanes pulled off onto the shoulder. He removed the Ohio plates and put the Jersey plates on and stowed the Ohio plates under the mat in the trunk. He smeared red Jersey mud on the bumpers and license plates, so the numbers could still be read but only with difficulty, and then turned around and drove north again, stopping at a motel in Linden. He borrowed some mucilage from the woman who ran the motel, attached the inspection sticker to the windshield of the Ford and went to bed.

5.

SITTING at the counter over a cup of coffee, Parker tried to figure out which waitress was Alma. Since it was Saturday, just after noon, the place was nearly full, and the four waitresses were kept constantly on the move. Parker watched them, one at a time, trying to decide.

One was soft-plump with frilly blonde hair and big blue eyes, the helpless magnolia-blossom type that works out best in the south and fails almost completely on the Jersey flats. Another was thin and stringy, with thin and stringy gray hair and a thin and stringy mouth; she surely had a school-age daughter or two at home, and her husband surely deserted her nine or ten years ago. The third was the German barmaid type, with sullen eyes and fat arms and a habit of throwing plates onto tables. The last was the horsy clumsy type, a young girl who couldn't stop thinking about sex; she got the orders wrong from all the male customers, and spent most of her nights knees-up on the back seats of Plymouths.

Parker studied them one by one, trying to decide. He crossed off the horsy nymphomaniac right away; when the armored car guards came in here for coffee and danish, that one would spend too much time thinking about their sex organs to wonder about the money they were guarding. The magnolia blossom might yearn for the goodies that money could bring, but if she were Alma she wouldn't offer Skimm any complicated plans for hitting the armored car—that type let the man do the thinking. The thin and stringy one had more than likely been married to a drifter who looked like Skimm, and she wouldn't trust him anyway since he was a man. And that left the German barmaid.

So that was Alma. She passed him, white waitress skirt rustling and nylons scraping together at the thighs, and went on down behind the counter to draw three cups of coffee. He watched her, frowning, not liking what he saw.

She was in her mid-thirties, and her waitress-short hair, a mousy brown in color, was crimped all around in a frizzy permanent. Her eyes were sullen and angry, glaring out at a world that had never given her her due. She was heavily built, with broad hips and full bosom and thick legs, all of it solid and hard. She had a double chin and a pulpy nose and a surprisingly good mouth, but the mouth was obscured by the hardness of the rest of her.

He looked at her, and he didn't like what he saw. There is no honor among thieves, perhaps, but there has to be trust among thieves when they're working together or they'll be too busy watching each other to watch what they're doing. And Parker didn't trust this Alma at all.

He watched her a while, seeing nothing to modify his opinion, then paid for his coffee and went out to the Ford. There was a Chevvy wagon parked in the spot where the armored car always stopped. Parker looked up and down the highway, wandered once around the parking lot, then climbed into the Ford and backed it out of its slot. He turned the wheel and drove around behind the diner, and saw the double dirt track angle off away from the parking lot through stubby undergrowth and occasional trees. He turned the Ford that way and followed the tracks up a gentle slope and down the other side. The road was in better condition than he'd expected. A car could make time on that road, and this would be important.

It was less than a mile north to the cross road, extravagantly called the Amboy Turnpike. Parker turned left and traveled a little more than five miles to Old Bridge. He didn't know where the deserted farmhouse was supposed to be, so he turned around and drove back north on the Amboy Turnpike again. This time he bypassed the road from the diner and kept on northward. Another mile brought him back to route 9, about half a mile north of the diner.

Less than five miles later, he left 9 on a long loop up to 440. Eastward on 440, it was three miles to Staten Island, via the Outerbridge Crossing. Parker stopped shy of the bridge, and pulled over against the curb. He smoked a Lucky as he watched the cars pass him and belt across the bridge. On the other side there was a toll booth construction across the road, built in California Mission style. Fourteen miles from there was the Staten Island Ferry, either to Manhattan or Brooklyn.

After a while he finished the cigarette, threw it out the window and turned the car around. He went back to 9, back to the Amboy Turnpike, back to Old Bridge. He parked outside a bar and pulled the New Jersey roadmap out of the glove compartment.

He studied it for a while, but there was no faster way to do it. In any kind of smash and grab, the object is to cross a state line as quickly as possible. The state where the crime took place is alerted first, with state police crawling over all the roads; it usually takes a while to get a neighboring state on its toes. If the states get along as badly as New Jersey and New York, it takes even longer.

He folded the map again, stowed it back in the glove compartment, and locked up the car. He went into the bar, drank draft beer for two hours and then looked up at the revolving Budweiser clock. "For God's sake," he said, "I've got to get to Brooklyn. What's the quickest way from here?"

"For Brooklyn?" The bartender thought it over. "You go out of here and take this street here straight out, to the left. That'll take you to route 9, and you take a left there till you see the sign for Outerbridge Crossing. That'll take you to Staten Island, and then you cross the Island and take the ferry."

"What if I take the Holland tunnel?"

"That's the long way around for Brooklyn, Mister. That'll lead you into Manhattan."

"Then that's the fastest way, huh? Go by Staten Island?"

"If you're going to Brooklyn."

"Thanks," said Parker. He left the bar and drove back to Newark.

6.

ACROSS the road from the diner there was a discount store in a concrete block building. At quarter after ten on Monday morning, Parker drove the Ford into the furniture store parking lot. There was cyclone fencing all around the blacktop parking lot, and Parker stopped the Ford with its nose to the fencing, facing the road. He could look straight out through the windshield at the diner across the way. He checked his watch, saw it wasn't twenty after ten yet, and lit a cigarette.

The armored car was red, and so short it looked stubby. It jounced into the diner lot at seventeen minutes to eleven, and stopped where Skimm had said it would. A Pontiac convertible was already there, in the spot between the armored car and the road.

Parker lit a fresh cigarette and watched. The driver got out, on the near side, and carefully closed the door behind him. He walked back the length of the truck and unlocked the rear door. The guard climbed out and waited while the driver locked the rear door again. Then the two of them walked into the diner.

Two minutes gone; fifteen minutes to eleven exactly.

They came back out at three minutes to eleven, and they both went to the rear of the truck. The driver unlocked the door, the guard climbed back in, the driver shut and locked the door again. Then he went back to the cab. The other guard opened the door for him from the inside, stepped down to the gravel, and the driver climbed up behind the wheel. The guard pushed the door closed and went into the diner.

He didn't take so long, probably because he didn't have anybody to talk to. At eight minutes after eleven, he came back out and went around to the far side of the armored car. The driver reached over and opened the door for him. He climbed in and the driver backed out of the space and bumped across the gravel to the concrete and headed south again on 9.

Parker got rolling right after him, coming out of the furniture store lot and heading north a quarter mile to the next place where he could make a U-turn. He hit sixty-five for a couple of minutes, coming back southward, and when he saw the red of the armored car far ahead of him he slowed down to fifty, matching the armored car's speed.

The road was four lanes wide for a while, and then it

narrowed down to two. There was very little traffic, only one Chevvy station wagon between Parker and the armored car. The wagon turned off on 520, and Parker hung back farther. He was watching the sides of the road and the road itself, but he didn't see anything that looked good. No blind turns, no hills, no valleys. The road was flat and straight, the curves wide and looping.

Parker quit before they reached Freehold, and turned the Ford around. He drove north a couple of miles and pulled onto the shoulder of the road. He shut the engine and got out of the car and opened the hood. Then he went back and sat behind the wheel again and lit a cigarette. He made himself comfortable in the seat and watched the rearview mirror.

A little after noon, a state patrol car pulled onto the shoulder just ahead of him, and a trooper got out looking like a modernized cowboy, only better fed. Parker rolled the window down and the trooper looked at him through his sunglasses and said, "Any trouble here?"

"She heated up," Parker answered. "My brother took a walk up to the Esso station for some water."

The trooper nodded. "That's all right, then."

"Thanks for stopping," Parker said.

The trooper hesitated, and then took one glove off. "May I see your license and registration, please?"

"I don't drive," Parker told him. "My brother drives. I'm just sitting over here till he comes back."

This was beginning to irritate him, but he didn't show it. The hood being up was supposed to answer all the questions, was supposed to keep cops from stopping to ask what he was parked on the shoulder for. But it was a dull day and a quiet road and not much traffic, so they'd stopped anyway—for the hell of it, to break the monotony.

"What about the registration?" the trooper asked.

"He's got that, too," Parker answered. "He keeps them both in his wallet."

"It's supposed to be in the car." The trooper wasn't suspicious or angry, just breaking the monotony. "He should have left it with you."

"I guess he didn't think," Parker said. He hoped the armored car wouldn't go by now, while he was bottled up with this idiot cop. "He was sore about the heating up and everything."

The trooper hesitated again, glancing through his sunglasses at the back seat. "How come he went for the water, instead of you? Seeing you don't drive."

Parker said, "I've got a game leg. That's why I can't get a driver's license."

The trooper was suddenly embarrassed. He pulled his glove back on and said, "You tell your brother about the registration."

"I will," Parker promised.

The trooper walked back to his own car, still looking like an overfed cowboy. He even had a rolling, slightly bowlegged walk. His black boots glistened in the sun. He got into the car and after a minute it pulled away and dwindled out of sight on the concrete road.

Parker watched it till it disappeared, and then lit a new cigarette and frowned at the rearview mirror.

That shouldn't have happened. To have a cop working the area of a job notice you, that was bad. The hood being up should have taken care of things; if the damn cop hadn't been bored, it would have. From now on, he'd have to watch two things at once, the job and that state trooper car. It wouldn't do for that trooper to see him driving.

He touched his fingers to his face, over his upper lip. His beard had been coming in spotty since the plastic surgery—the doctor had said that would straighten out after a while—but the hair on the upper lip grew the same as always. It might not be a bad idea to grow a moustache. If the same cop stopped him again, he could be his own brother. Amazing family resemblance. Parker grinned sourly at the thought, still watching the rearview mirror.

He saw the red in the mirror at twenty after one, coming like a bat out of hell. He got out of the Ford and closed the hood and was getting back behind the wheel when the armored car went by. He started the engine and took off after it. The armored car was staying between fifty-five and sixty now; these guys were probably quitting work as soon as they reported in. Watching for the trooper's car, Parker stayed with the red tin box, without getting too close.

They went by the Shore Points Diner and over the Raritan River and straight on up 9—four lanes all the way now—to Elizabeth. When the armored car turned off, in town, Parker kept going straight, on up to Newark. He'd seen all he wanted to see. The diner was where it would have to be done. There wasn't any place at all along the road where they could flag it for the toby, so that meant they'd have to use Alma.

Parker didn't like it. First Alma, and then the bored cop. It was beginning to smell sour. There were too many things to watch, all at once. But he needed the stake, so he'd go to the Green Rose tonight, but if the job got any more sour anywhere along the line he'd drop it. He was figuring on splitting half, plus the bankroller's cut, and that made it a boodle worth going after.

In Newark, he parked on a side street. He had time to kill, so he went to a movie. It was the fourth double feature he'd seen since Saturday.

7.

THE Green Rose was oblong, and very dim. A trough high around the wall contained indirect lighting, alternate red and green lengths of fluorescent tubes. Some of the mechanical beer and whisky display ads on the bar back were lighted, and there was a light over the cash register, but the rest of the place was like a tomb.

Coming in the door, the dark mahogany bar was to the left, extending back to the wall projection for the rest rooms. Booths with dark red leather seats and black formica on the tables were on the right. Parker walked down the line between the bar and the booths to the back, where there was a bigger booth across from the rest rooms. They were there, all three of them.

Skimm and Alma sat facing the front of the bar, with Alma on the outside, so she'd been to the head already. They both had beer in front of them, a glass and a thin bottle and a glass and a thin bottle, and Alma's glass and bottle were almost empty. Handy McKay was sitting on the other side, half-turned, with his back against the wall.

He was long and thin and made of gristle, and his stiff dark hair was gray over the ears. He lipped his cigarettes so badly the brown tobacco showed through the paper for half an inch, and he used wooden matches, the little ones, not the big kitchen matches. Whenever he got cigarettes from a machine, he threw the pack of paper matches away. Between cigarettes, he poked at his teeth with the plain end of one of the wooden matches.

"Hello, Handy. Move your knee."

Handy turned his head slowly and raised an eyebrow

29

at Skimm. Skimm grinned, though otherwise he was acting nervous. "That's Parker."

"Son of a bitch," said Handy thoughtfully. He moved his knee and watched Parker sit down. "Did a good job on you," he said.

"Yeah."

Alma said suddenly, "You were in the diner Saturday." Her voice was harsh, but low.

Parker looked at her. "That's right."

Skimm was very nervous. "Parker, this is Alma. Alma, Parker." He looked at them both as though he wanted to say, "Don't fight."

Alma turned to Skimm, "We need more beer. How come he was in the diner Saturday?"

"Looking it over," said Skimm. "Here comes the bartender now. He had to look the setup over first, ain't that right, Parker?"

Parker nodded. Skimm ordered four more bottles of Bud and the bartender went away.

"It's a good setup," Parker said.

"Like I told you," Skimm answered. He sounded relieved, but still nervous.

"You figure just the four of us, Parker?"

"It's a small pie, Handy," Parker replied.

"I want to talk about that." Alma said. She seemed ready for a fight about anything.

"Not here," Parker said.

There was a cigarette in the ashtray that had been lipped very badly. Handy picked it up and said, "I haven't seen you in a while, Parker."

"Few years," Parker answered.

"What do you hear from Stanton?"

"He went to jail a couple years ago. Out in Indiana."

Handy puffed thoughtfully on his cigarette, holding it from force of habit in his cupped fingers so the light wouldn't show. "How'd it happen?"

"They shot his gas tank as he pulled away from the bank. It didn't blow, but it drained out before he could make the switch. He tried walking to the other car, and they picked him up. Three of them, Stanton and Beak Weiss and one other guy."

Handy shook his head. "Bad."

"It wouldn't of happened," Parker said quietly, "but their driver ditched while they were in the bank. A kid, new at the game." He glanced at Skimm, and back to Handy. "That held them up, having to start the car."

"You got to be careful who you work with," Handy said. He put his cigarette out, bending the lipped end onto the ember, making a small fizzing sound.

The bartender brought the new round and Skimm paid. He was more nervous than ever. They waited while he counted out change and added a bill. The bartender scooped it off the formica and went away, and Skimm said, bright and nervous, "This is a nice place, Parker. You picked a nice place." Beside him, Alma was glaring, still ready for the fight.

They sat there and drank the beer, and Parker and Handy talked about people they knew. Skimm sat stiff, elbows on the table, not quite bouncing up and down, with a nervous grin on his face. He wanted to talk with them, because he knew most of the same people, but he didn't want Alma to feel left out, so he didn't talk, just smiled and grinned and looked nervous.

When they finished the beer, Parker said to Skimm, "You got a place in town?"

"In Irvington. It ain't far."

"We'll go there."

They went outside to the sidewalk and Parker said, "You got a car?"

Alma answered. "Over there, the green Dodge."

"I'll follow you." Parker turned to Handy. "You got a car?"

"No."

"Ride along with me."

They walked down the street. Parker's car was down at the end of the block, facing the wrong way. They got in, and he made a U-turn and waited till the green Dodge passed him. Alma was driving. They could see her mouth moving, angry talk, and Skimm looking worried. Parker pulled out behind the Dodge and followed it to Springfield Avenue and down Springfield toward Irvington.

When they'd ridden a few blocks, Handy said, "She's going to try a cross."

"I know that."

Handy nodded. "I figured you did." He pulled a box of matches out of his pocket, took one of the matches, and poked at his teeth with it. He held the box in his other hand and shook it a little, to make the matches rattle inside. "So then what?"

"We split two ways," Parker said.

Handy grunted. "What about Skimm?"

"Either she's talked him over, or she figures to bump him."

"Why not do it without her?"

"She's the finger, she could finger us. Besides, we need her in the setup. She blinds one side during the job."

Handy nodded, and kept poking at his teeth. "You got the cross figured?"

Parker nodded. "I'll take you over the route."

They rode a while longer, and Handy said, "You nervous, Parker?"

"There's too much to watch. I don't like this Alma thing. If it gets worse, I pull out."

"I'll go with you."

They followed the green Dodge when it turned off Springfield Avenue. They drove along secondary streets a while. Handy lit a new cigarette, using the match he'd been poking against his teeth. "I been meaning to ask you about something."

When he didn't go on, Parker said, "What?"

"I heard you was dead. I heard your wife done it. Then Skimm told me you done your wife in, and the syndicate was after you."

"Outfit," said Parker.

"What?"

"They call it the Outfit. I was in an operation that went sour. This guy Mal, you wouldn't know him, he put Lynn in a squeeze. Either she dropped me or he'd drop her. She did her best, and this guy Mal thought it was good enough. Then he went to New York and used my share to pay off an old debt to the Outfit. They took him on in some kind of job, and when I got on my feet I settled him and got my money back from the Outfit."

Handy grunted again. It was the way he laughed. "They didn't like it much, huh?"

"I had to louse up their business day a little bit."

"What about your wife? Lynn. I heard you settled with her, too."

Parker shook his head. "I wanted to, but I didn't. When she found she hadn't done me, she killed herself."

Handy grunted. "Saved you the trouble, huh?"

Parker shrugged. He'd wanted to kill her, to even things, but when he'd seen her he'd known he couldn't. She was the only one he'd ever met that he didn't feel simply about. With everybody else in the world, the situation was simple. They were in and he worked with them or they were out and he ignored them or they were trouble and he took care of them. But with Lynn he hadn't been able to work that way.

He'd felt for her what he'd never felt for anybody else or anything else, not even himself, not even money. She had tried her level best to kill him, and even that hadn't changed anything, the way he felt about her or his helplessness with her. He didn't want that to happen again, ever, to feel about anybody that way, to let his feelings get stronger than his judgment. Oddly enough, he missed her and wished she were still alive and still with him, even though he knew that sooner or later she would have found herself in the same kind of bind again and done the same thing.

Ahead of him, the green Dodge turned into a driveway next to a small faded clapboard house. This was an old section here; all the houses were small and faded—most of them with sagging porches.

There was no garage. The green Dodge turned into the backyard and stopped. Parker pulled up beside it, and he and Handy got out. Alma and Skimm were waiting for them, by the back door. There were three warped steps up, and a small back porch half the width of the house. The kitchen door had masking tape over a break in the window. Skimm lived in places where broken things were patched with masking tape.

They all went into the kitchen and Alma told Skimm to open up some beer.

"Sure," said Skimm. He wasn't nervously happy any more, he was sullen now.

Alma told the others to come on into the living room. She'd argued most of the belligerence out on the drive. She was sure of herself now, and in charge.

They went through the dining room, going around a scarred table. The house was one story high, with a living room and a dining room and a kitchen and two bedrooms. One bedroom was off the dining room and the other one was off the kitchen. The bathroom was off the kitchen on the other side, next to the steps to the basement.

Alma clicked a wall switch and a ceiling light went on, four forty-watt bulbs amid a cluster of stained glass. Alma led the way into the room. "Look at this lousy place. Just look at it."

It wasn't very good. The sofa was green mohair, worn smooth in some places and spiny in others. The two arm-chairs both rested the weight of their springs on the floor, and one of them had an old deep cigarette burn in one overstuffed arm. The rug was faded and worn, showing trails where people had done the most walking, to the front door and the dining room archway. There was an old television set with an eleven-inch screen and a wooden cabinet with a folded matchbook under one leg.

Alma pulled the wrinkled shades down over the three living room windows. "Sit down."

Parker and Handy took the armchairs. Skimm came in, carrying four cans of beer, and passed them around. Then he and Alma sat on the sofa.

Alma started. "Skimm tells me you don't like the plan."

"Did he tell you why?" Parker asked.

"I don't mean the tear gas," she said. "The rest of it."

"Which rest of it?" Parker asked.

"We need five men," she said. "We can't do it with less. For God's sake, it's an armored car."

"You want to lay a siege and starve them out?" Parker asked.

"Don't be a wise guy."

Handy didn't have a cigarette going, he had a match poked into his mouth. He took it out and said, "Who's running this operation?"

Nobody answered him. Parker looked at Skimm, and Skimm looked at the floor. Alma looked at Handy.

Handy pointed the wet end of the match at Alma. "You're the finger." He pointed the match at Skimm. "You brung us in. You running it, Skimm?"

Skimm looked up, reluctantly. "I never worked an armored car before."

"I ain't running it," said Handy. "I'm not the type. So that leaves Parker."

Parker said, "I don't like this situation. More and more,

I don't like it. The finger sitting in, doing a lot of talking.
I just don't like it."

"I've got a stake in this too, you know," Alma said.
She was getting hot again, a slow flush creeping up her
face.

"Skimm, who's running this operation?" Parker asked.

Skimm was even more reluctant to answer this time.
When he finally spoke, it was to Alma. "Parker knows this
kind of job."

Alma said, "Let's hear what he has to say."

"It's simple. Three men. One in a uniform like the
guards wear. We get the two trucks, and one car. One of
the trucks we rig up so we can lock the guards in it, keep
them cooled for a while. The driver and the guard from
the back go in first. While they're in the diner, we get in
position. When they come out, we grab them at the back
of the armored car, where the other guard in the cab can't
see us. We wait till they open the back door. Then we
grab them, and the one in the uniform takes the driver up
to the cab. The guard inside opens the door when he
recognizes the driver, and the other one—that's one of
us—hangs back, so the guard'll just glimpse the uniform
out of the corner of his eye. He opens up, and we've got
him, too. We sap all three of them and lock them in the
truck. Then we transfer the cash and take off in the car.
We leave the trucks there because we don't need them
any more."

"That's what I don't like," said Alma. "That's the part
I don't like."

Parker drank some beer and looked at her.

"They're going to see your car," Alma said. "It's going
to be at the back of the U, blocking vision, so they're going to see it. That's why I wanted the trucks to be in it,
too. We'd have vehicles going off in all different directions
and they wouldn't know which way to go to look for us."

It didn't matter which way they went, or how many

people saw them go. Parker knew that but he didn't say anything about it. This Alma was a busher, a new fish, she didn't know how this kind of operation was handled. Parker knew this, because it was his line of work, but he didn't say anything about it. All he said was, "Tractor-trailers don't outrun police cars. We leave them at the diner."

"I still want cars going off in different directions."

Parker nodded. He knew why she wanted it, but she didn't know he knew. He said, "So what's your idea?"

"My car," she said, "my car, that's the Dodge out there. It'll be parked behind the diner, like always. When you get the money out of the armored car, you put it in my car. Then you take off on route 9, going south, and circle around back to Old Bridge. When I know the job's finished, I'll get in my car and take the back road. Then we meet at the farmhouse outside Old Bridge. That way, even if you get stopped they've got nothing on you because you aren't carrying the money."

Parker glanced at Skimm. He was studying the carpet, lines of worry creasing his forehead. Parker said to Alma, "I don't like it. That leaves you holding the cash, and the rest of us holding the bag. I know Skimm, and I trust him, and I know Handy, but I don't know you."

"So one of you rides with me," she said. "Skimm. He can ride with me. All right?"

It was bad. The whole idea was stupid. It was sloppy, it was bad business.

But Parker nodded. "That's all right. Just so one of us goes along with the money."

If he let her keep her original plan he could be sure of getting the money back. If he forced her to change by making the grab more sensible, then maybe he wouldn't be able to figure out her cross in time. He'd had to argue so she wouldn't get suspicious. The only one he had to worry about was Skimm. Skimm, if he was thinking sensibly, had to know the two-car scheme was nonsense. He would have to wonder why Parker was going along with it. If Alma had talked him into her plans, that would make him dangerous because he'd realize that Parker was onto the cross. But it made more sense that Alma was playing a lone game, that she was figuring to cross Skimm, too.

"What about bankrolling?" Handy asked.

"I got it," Parker said. "Three grand." He pulled a long white envelope from his jacket pocket. "I brought five C with me," he said, "in case there was any need for it."

Handy nodded. "You going to equip us?"

"Yes."

"Then I don't need any."

Alma was staring at the envelope. "Skimm could use some money," she said.

"This isn't for personal expenses. This is bankrolling. That means to buy what we need for the operation."

Skimm said, in a small voice, "I don't need any."

Parker put the envelope back in his pocket. Alma watched it disappear, a vertical anger line between her brows. Parker asked, "Is there anything else?"

Alma blinked, and said, "When do we do it? Next Monday?"

"Dry run next Monday. The week after that, maybe, if it looks right. Or the week after that. Whenever it looks right."

"I don't want too much delay," Alma said.

Parker got to his feet. "We do the job when we know it'll come off right. That's why we don't go to jail." He turned to Handy. "I'll give you a lift."

Handy stood up. "Fine."

Parker turned back to Skimm. "You got a phone?"

"Yeah. Clover 5-7598."

"I'll give you a call."

"All right." Skimm looked at Parker for just a second, and then his eyes slid away. He still looked worried.

Parker drained the beer can and tossed it into the chair he'd just left. "Nice to meet you, Alma."

She struggled, and said, "Nice to meet you, too."

Parker and Handy walked through the house to the kitchen and out the back door. They got into the Ford and drove out to the street, and Handy said, "I've got a room in Newark."

"Right," Parker said. He headed back toward Springfield Avenue.

Handy poked at his teeth with a match. After a while, he said, "That's garbage, that stuff."

"About the two cars?"

"Yeah."

"You know why I went along."

"You've got her figured."

Parker nodded. "I wonder where Skimm is."

"I've always trusted that little bastard," said Handy. "We worked together a couple times. Once in Florida, once in Oklahoma."

"I never work in Florida," said Parker. "I play there."

"You got a good system." He poked at his teeth some more. Then he said, "I'd like to know about Skimm, though."

"I don't think he's in it. She's got him tight, but not that tight. She figures to cross him too, and take the whole pie for herself."

"That poor bastard."

"You want to wise him?"

Handy considered, the match working in his mouth. "I don't know," he said. "He'll be in the car with her."

"He wouldn't believe you." Parker shrugged. "You fall in love with a woman, you've got a blind spot."

Handy glanced at him, and away. "I suppose." They rode a while longer and then he said, "You think she'll bump him?"

"Yeah."

"Maybe she'll flub it. Then Skimm's got the boodle."

"He'll split." Parker shrugged. "Skimm's getting old. Old and worried. I don't think she'll flub it."

"That poor bastard."

"He'll be better off," Parker said. "Hooked the way he is."

"I suppose so."

They rode a while longer, and then Handy said, "I wish it was simple, Parker. I wish to Christ it was simple. Can you remember the last time a job was simple?"

"A long time ago."

"It sounds like a good setup." Handy reached for his cigarettes. "The way you talked about it, it sounds fine. But there's this Alma." He lit the new cigarette, lipping it. "There's always an Alma. Every damn time. Why can't we put together a job without an Alma in it?"

"I don't know," Parker said. He was thinking of a guy named Mal, the reason he'd had to change his face.

Handy sat for a while, thinking. "This is the last one for me."

"Uh huh," said Parker. There was an Alma in every job, an Alma or a Mal or whatever the name was. And there was a Handy in every job, too. There was always one that was ready to quit; this was the last job and he was going to take the dough from this one and buy a chicken farm or something and settle down. There was a Handy in every job, and he always showed up for a job again a year or two later.

Thinking about it, it surprised him that there were always the same people in every job. There was always one that had to be watched, like Alma. There was always one who was quitting after this grab, and this time it was Handy. And there was always one who had probably a hundred thousand dollars to his name, buried in fields and forests here and there across the country in tin cans and metal boxes, and this one was probably Skimm. Skimm always looked and acted like a bum, so he was probably the kind that buried it, buried it all.

Parker had known others like that, there was one in almost every operation. They took their share and peeled off of it two or three thousand, just enough to carry them for a while, and then they went off by themselves somewhere and buried the rest of it. They figured to dig it up again some day, but they never did. The day never got rainy enough and that was why bulldozer operators working on new housing developments every once in a while turned up a metal box with thirty or forty thousand dollars in it.

After a while, Handy said, "You turn right the next corner."

They turned right, and the car behind them turned right, too.

Parker watched it in the rearview mirror and said, "Son of a bitch."

It didn't make any sense, and that bothered him.

The next street was one way the wrong way, but the one after that Parker made a left. So did the car behind him. He went two blocks and made a right and then another right and then a left. The car stayed with him. He drove along until he saw a "Dead End Street" sign and turned into it. He slowed down to almost a crawl, going around the corner, and stayed slow like that, so the car behind him came around the corner and was all of a sudden a lot closer.

It was a short street, with a railroad embankment crossing it at the end. The street was a kind of valley, with the houses on high land on either side, stone or concrete steps leading up from the sidewalk to the house level.

Parker turned into a driveway on the right, going very slowly, the Ford straining against going up the steep slope of the driveway so slowly. The other car went on by, down toward the embankment. Parker pushed the clutch in suddenly, and the car rolled back down the embankment and out across the street. It was a narrow street; with the parked cars, the Ford blocked it completely.

"Back me," Parker said.

He left the motor running, and pulled the emergency brake on. Then he got out of the Ford and walked down to the end of the street, where the other car was stopped facing the embankment. It was a black Lincoln. Looking through the rear window as he walked forward, Parker could see the driver alone in the car. He came around the lefthand side, and opened the door.

Stubbs was wearing his chauffeur's costume, complete with hat, and he was holding a .45. He pointed it at Parker, and said, "Hold it right there!"

Parker stood where he was, with his hand still on the door handle.

Stubbs said, "I got to know where you was Saturday."

Parker kept looking at Stubbs, not to the right where Handy was crawling along the pavement, coming up alongside the car, keeping low out of Stubbs' range of vision.

"What for?" Parker asked.

"The doc was killed Saturday," Stubbs said. "One of you bastards did it."

"I was here in Jersey," said Parker, as Handy reached up and plucked the automatic out of Stubbs' hand. Parker leaned in and clipped him on the side of the neck. While Stubbs was getting over that, Handy got to his feet pointing the automatic. "Get out of the car."

Stubbs got out, holding his neck. "You better not kill me," he said. "If May don't hear from me, she sends letters about your new face."

It irritated Parker, another useless complication. He slid in behind the wheel of the Lincoln and parked it in an open slot by the embankment. Then he came back and said to Handy, "Your place?"

"It's the closest."

They put Stubbs in the front seat of the Ford, next to Parker, who was driving. Handy sat in the back seat, watching Stubbs, the automatic in his lap. He gave Parker directions the rest of the way to his place.

Handy had a room in a building that had started out as a private home and then become a boarding house and now was just a place with furnished rooms. But the furniture was clean, and not quite as ugly as at Skimm's place.

The phone was out in the hall. They stood there, Handy holding the automatic in Stubbs' back, while Parker dialed Skimm's place. The ring came in his ear three times, and then Skimm answered, sounding sleepy. Parker told him who it was. "Alma there?"

Skimm hesitated. "Yes. She was just leaving."

"Sure. I got somebody here I want her to talk to. He'll ask her when she saw me in the diner. It's okay for her to tell him."

"What's going on, Parker?"

"I'll tell you sometime. Put Alma on."

"Okay, wait a second." There was mumbling, away from the phone, and then Alma came on the line. She sounded snappish.

"Hold on," said Parker. "Tell this guy when I was in the diner." He handed the phone to Stubbs.

Stubbs took the phone, frowning in concentration. It was getting too complicated for his battered brain. He said, "Hello? What time Saturday? Where is this diner?"

After that he frowned some more, staring heavily at the phone box on the wall, until he said, in answer to something from Alma, "I'm thinking," and hung up.

"You happy?" Parker asked.

Stubbs turned around, looking like somebody trying to answer a tough question. "She says you was in there around noon."

"That's right."

"The Doc was killed maybe four o'clock in the afternoon, while I was washing the cars."

Parker shook his head, disgusted. "You know how far Nebraska is from here?"

Stubbs chewed on that for a while and then said, "Okay, it wasn't you." That settled, he turned to Handy. "Gimme the gun back, will ya?"

Handy looked at Parker, wondering if this clown was kidding. "Just wait a minute, Stubbs. I think we've got to talk."

"Sure," said Handy. He held onto the automatic.

"There's nothing to talk about. You didn't do it."

"This way," said Handy. He motioned with the automatic.

Stubbs wanted to argue some more, but Parker hit him openhanded on the ear, where a punchy could feel it. Stubbs screwed his face up and hunched his shoulder and cupped his hand over his ear, and then he went where Handy told him.

They walked into the apartment, and Parker told Stubbs to sit down on the leather chair. Handy sat over to the side, in the maroon overstuffed chair, and Parker stood in the middle of the brown rug. He looked at Stubbs for a while, and then he made a disgusted sound. "All right. Now what?"

"I don't know what you mean," Stubbs said. His face was still screwed up, and his hand was still up protecting his ear. "I'm willing to go."

"That's it," Parker said. "Go where?"

"I got two more suspects."

Parker nodded. "That's what I thought." He went over to the sofa and sat down and lit a cigarette. "All right, tell me about it."

"The Doc only did three jobs in the last year," Stubbs said. "We figured it has to be one of them three, or the guy wouldn't have waited so long. If it was a guy from two years ago, see, and he was going to go for the Doc, he'd of done it already."

"You and May," said Parker. "You worked that out?"

"May, mostly," Stubbs answered. "I figured, I got to get the guy. There's nobody else to do it, because the Doc was a Red."

Parker glanced at Handy, and shook his head. Handy shrugged. From listening, he was beginning to understand.

"And if May doesn't hear from you, she blows the whistle, is that it?"

"Yeah."

"On who?"

"The last three. She wouldn't be able to know which one it was, which one got me. So she'd blow the whistle on the last three."

"Including me," said Parker.

"But you didn't do it," said Stubbs, frowning. He'd missed something somewhere. "You're out of it, you didn't do it."

"What if number two did it?" Parker asked. "And instead of you getting him, he gets you. Then May blows the whistle on me. Right?"

Stubbs hadn't thought of that. He frowned heavily, scrubbing his hand over his face. Then he brightened a little. "Don't you worry. He won't get me, I'll get him."

Handy laughed. He tossed Stubbs' gun in the air and caught it. "The way you got Parker?"

Stubbs looked at him, not understanding, and Parker explained. "He knew me by the name of Anson," he said to Handy.

"Oh."

Parker said, "Listen, Stubbs. What if you phone May and tell her I'm in the clear?"

Stubbs shook his head. "We talked about that. How it could be faked, maybe. She's got to see me in person."

"God damn it," Parker said, "I don't have time for this crap."

Handy shrugged. "You'll have to go back to Nebraska with him."

"I don't have time," said Parker angrily. "The job's set up for two weeks from now. We've got to set up the cars, the routes, we've got to chart the state troopers, we've got to buy guns—" He mashed his cigarette out and got to his feet. "There's too much to do. Stubbs, when's the deadline?"

Stubbs blinked at him. "What?"

"The deadline, the deadline. When does May blow the whistle if she doesn't hear from you?"

"Oh. A month from now. From yesterday. Four weeks from yesterday."

Parker paced back and forth, looking down at the carpet. "Two days," he said. "Even if we fly out. One day out and one day back. Two days for Alma to fast-talk Skimm, two days with nothing getting done."

"We could hold the job off for a week."

Parker shook his head. "It's sour enough already. I want to get it over with. Another week for Alma to think up some more cute ideas? Another week for that damn cop to see me driving by?"

"What cop?"

Parker shrugged. He didn't feel like talking about it. "A cop paid attention to me on route 9."

"Near the diner?"

"South of it." He turned and studied Stubbs. "The easiest thing," he said, "would be to bump you and drop you in a pool by one of the refineries. Then two weeks from now I go cut May."

Stubbs doggedly shook his head. "She's got her common-law husband with her," he said. "And his brother. They figure something might happen like that."

"What if you just let him go?"

"Look at him," Parker said. "He's punchy. He goes up against the guy who killed that doctor, he's dead. Then I'm dead."

"I can take care of myself," Stubbs said.

"Sure," Parker answered.

"So what do you want to do?" Handy asked.

"There's too much to watch. I'm ready to pull out of this damn thing, there's too much to watch."

"I could use the cash," Handy said. "This is my last job, you know."

"Yeah. That's the thing, I need it too." Parker looked at Stubbs and shook his head. "I've got to hold onto this beetle for two weeks. I've got to put him on ice."

Handy considered that. "What about the farm?"

"What farm?"

"Outside Old Bridge. Where we're supposed to meet after the job. You been out there yet?"

"Not yet."

"We could stash him there, maybe."

Parker thought about it. So many things to watch. The job, Alma, the state trooper, and now Stubbs. But he didn't have anything else on the fire. "That's a bad way to work it. To hang around the hideout before the job."

"Do you figure we're going there after it?"

"That's right. I forgot about Alma." Parker shrugged. "All right. We'll put him on ice out there."

Handy stood up, and waved the automatic at Stubbs. "Come along."

Stubbs said, "Listen, what are you trying to pull?"

"Look," Parker said. "Look at him, he wants to argue."

Handy turned to Stubbs. "How's your kneecaps? In good shape?"

Stubbs caught the message. He got to his feet and shut up. They took him downstairs and back to the Ford. They drove over to 9 and headed south, Parker driving, with Stubbs beside him and Handy in the back seat.

On the way Parker asked, "How'd you get to me?"

"That letter you got," Stubbs said. "I looked up that Lasker fella in Cincinnati, and he left a forwarding address. I went there and hung around till I saw you."

"He left a forwarding address," repeated Parker. He shook his head and kept driving. He didn't know if this was Handy's last job, but he knew it was Skimm's.

TWO

◆◆◆◆◆◆◆◆◆◆◆

I.

PARKER left the car off Hudson Boulevard in Jersey City and walked two blocks to the office building. There were two elevators, but only one of them was working. An ancient angular Negro with a loose vacant smile operated it. Its metal sides were painted green, and there were grease smears on the doors.

Parker got out on the third floor and turned left. A sign on the fourth door down read: "Eastern Agency Confidential Investigations." He pushed the door open and went into a small green reception room. On one wall was a certificate stating that James Lawson was a licensed private investigator.

A bleached blonde, looking secondhand, sat at the gray metal desk, talking on the phone. When Parker came in she said, "Hold on, Marge." She pressed the telephone to her hard breast and looked at Parker.

"Doctor Hall to see Lawson." Parker said.

"One moment, please." She told Marge to hold on

again, and got up and went to the door of the inner office. She had stripper's hips, big and thick and wrapped in a tight black skirt. She went through into the inner office, and in a minute she came back. "Go right on in, Doctor."

"Thanks," said Parker.

She went back to her desk and her phone call, and Parker went through to the inner office and closed the door.

James Lawson was small and balding. He looked like the kind of man who was worried about being out of condition, who kept promising himself he'd start going to a gym but never went. He looked across his wooden desk at Parker. "I don't think I know you."

Lawson wasn't a man to trust with the new face. "Parker sent me. Him and Handy McKay."

"So you can name-drop," said Lawson. "Doctor Hall, and Parker, and Handy McKay. Parker's dead."

"No, he ain't. Him and Handy and Pete Skimm and me are working on a job. You want to call Skimm?"

Lawson shook his head. "I don't call anybody," he said. "Where'd you get the Dr. Hall from?"

"Parker. He said I should call myself Doctor Hall, and then you'd know what was what."

"How come he didn't come himself?"

"He can't show himself in the East. He ran into trouble with the Outfit."

Lawson nodded. "I heard something about that, too. But I also heard he was dead."

"He wasn't, the last time I talked to him."

Lawson chewed on a knuckle. "You look okay," he said, "and you sound okay. But I don't know you."

"Do you think I'm law? If I was law, I wouldn't play games. I could take your license away without half trying. I wouldn't have to fool around with you."

"Take my license away for what?"

"For the time you gave Parker the three Magnums and the Positive."

Lawson started. "You know about that?"

"Parker told me. So let's quit fooling around."

"Maybe I better call Skimm," said Lawson. He was suddenly very nervous.

Parker gave him the number, and then sat down in the client's chair during the phone call. Skimm was home, and Parker had already told him the right answers. Lawson talked with him briefly, and then hung up.

"You ready to deal?"

."Sure." Lawson grinned, his lips wet. "But I ought to know who I'm dealing with." he said.

"Flynn. Joe Flynn."

"I don't think I've heard of you."

"I've always worked out around the Coast before this."

"And where's this job? Here in Jersey?"

Parker shook his head. "Youngstown, Ohio," he said. "You'll read about it in the papers."

Lawson was a man you could trust, so long as you never told him anything.

Lawson opened a drawer and took out a pencil and notepad. "What do you need?"

"Three guns. Medium size—.32's or .38's."

Lawson nodded. "I'll look around. Anything else?"

"Two trucks. Semis."

"Tractor-trailers?" Lawson frowned, and tapped his pencil point against the notepad. "That's a tricky one. There isn't so much market in those big ones any more. That'll probably cost you."

Parker shrugged. "If it costs too much, we'll steal our own."

Lawson tapped the pencil faster against the notepad. "You've still got the registration to worry about. And the cover."

"Don't need them," Parker said. "Just the trucks."

"Stripped?"

"It doesn't matter."

"Oh. That isn't so tough, then. I know one already, if it isn't sold. Down in North Carolina. I'll check on it for you." He wrote on the notepad again. "Anything else?"

"Some place to get some work done on one of the trucks."

"Engine or body?"

"Body."

Lawson nodded. "I think I know the place for you. Anything else?"

"No." Parker got to his feet. "That's all we need. You can leave messages with Skimm."

Lawson ripped the top page from the notepad, stuffed it in his side pocket. "You ought to leave something with me. Sort of a drawing account."

Parker took out his wallet, peeled off four fifties, and dropped them on Lawson's desk.

Lawson picked them up and grinned. "You want a receipt? You know, for tax purposes?"

"No," Parker said. "Leave the word with Skimm."

"Will do."

Parker went back downstairs in the green elevator and walked back to the Ford. It had a parking ticket on it. He threw the ticket into the gutter and drove away, back to Hudson Boulevard and then to the Pulaski Skyway and down 9. Because of the trooper, and not wanting to be near the diner too soon before the job, he turned on 1 when it branched away to the right. At New Brunswick, he turned left on 18, then right at Old Bridge, heading down toward Spotswood. But before he got there he turned left up a winding dirt road.

The land here was red clay and white sand mixed together, with a fuzz of wild gray grass and here and there thick-trunked trees. The road seemed to end shortly but Parker went up an overgrown slope, and the dirt road angled sharply around a tree and then dropped away down the dip into a kind of cup.

Down in the indentation stood a gray farmhouse, nearly invisible on days the sun didn't shine. Someone had once tried to make the land grow something besides wild grasses and occasional trees. But the farmhouse was slowly rotting away now, becoming a part of the land. It couldn't be seen from any road, and most people in the area probably didn't even know it existed. The dirt road leading in was sometimes used as a lover's lane, but those people never even came in very far. They didn't care what was over the slope; they just wanted not to be seen from the road.

When Parker had first come, the road had been impassable. The turn around the tree at the top of the slope had been choked with underbrush and dead branches. They would not have cleared it until the day before the job, but now there was Stubbs, so Parker had hacked away at it with an ax and cleared enough room for the Ford to just get through. He made it now on the first try and came down the grassed-over double track on the other side.

He drove around to the back of the farmhouse, left the Ford up close against the house—he would have liked to park it in the barn, but that had already fallen in—and went down the steps into the basement. The flooring upstairs was unsafe, so they used only the basement.

It didn't smell like a basement. The windows were all broken out, and sand had sifted in over the years. It smelled mummified. There were two cots set up along one wall, a card table and three folding chairs on the other side, and a camp stove by the ruins of the furnace so the smoke would go up the chimney.

Parker went over to the door to the fruit cellar and hit it with his fist. "You in there?"

Stubbs' voice came through the thick door faintly. "Go to hell."

Parker took the bar down and went back to the card table, where the automatic lay next to the canned goods. He picked up the automatic and called, "Come on out."

There was a pause, and the door pushed slightly open. Another pause, and the door jolted back and slammed against the wall and Stubbs came out with a gray chunk of two-by-four lifted over his head.

Parker motioned with the automatic. He watched Stubbs decide whether or not to throw the two-by-four at him, but Stubbs decided against it. When he dropped it, Parker said, "Let's go out in the air."

He would rather have just left Stubbs locked away in the fruit cellar for two weeks, but if he did Stubbs might get sick and die. He couldn't afford yet to have Stubbs die. He had to waste some time now getting Stubbs out in the sunlight.

They went outside and Parker sat down on the ground, his back against the wall of the farmhouse. "Go on, walk around a little," he said.

Stubbs stood blinking in the light. There was no window in the fruit cellar, and he'd been in pitch-dark. He looked around, blinking in the light. "I got to go."

"Over there." Parker pointed with the automatic. "Away from the house, over by that tree there. And cover it up."

Stubbs stood around, undecided. "I'm out of cigarettes."

Parker tossed him his pack, and some matches. He had more in the glove compartment of the Ford. Stubbs picked them up from where they'd fallen at his feet, and slowly lit a cigarette. He stuffed the pack and the matches in his pants pocket and looked sullenly at Parker. "You can't kidnap me like this."

Parker shrugged. It didn't need an answer.

Stubbs screwed his face up, the way he did when he was trying to think. He wanted to tell Parker this whole thing was impossible, you just don't lock a man away in a fruit cellar for two weeks with no electricity and no plumbing. But Parker was doing it, and that didn't leave Stubbs much to say. After a minute, he turned and trudged over toward the tree.

They stayed outside for half an hour, and then they went back into the basement and Parker let Stubbs make himself some beans and instant coffee at the camp stove. There was bread, too, but no butter, and a can of peaches for dessert. Stubbs thought about tossing a can of beans at Parker's head, but Parker told him to forget about it, so Stubbs forgot about it.

After he'd cleaned up his dinner utensils, Parker let him go outside again for a while. Then he put him back in the fruit cellar, put the bar across the door. "I'll see you tomorrow," he called through the door.

There wasn't any answer, so Parker shrugged and walked away. It was just about sundown, darker in the cup around the farmhouse than up along the ridge. Parker got into the Ford, started the engine, and drove carefully through the dusk back to the road. He turned right and drove back toward the motel where he was staying, stopping off at a diner for a chicken dinner.

Handy showed up a little after ten in Alma's green Dodge. Alma didn't like him using it, but he needed it for the stakeout and after a while she'd given in. He'd spent the day and part of the evening at various spots on route 9 working out the state trooper beats. They talked it over for a while, and then Parker said, "Let Skimm take over Thursday. I want to show you the doublecross."

Handy nodded. "I've been thinking about that."

Then they went out to a nearby bar and drank some beer. After a while they split, and Parker went back to the motel. He was in bed by one o'clock.

2.

PARKER slowed as he neared the toll booths, and fumbled in his pocket for change. The toll booth structure was pale stucco with a green California Mission roof. It should have been on a road in Italy or Spain, rather than at the eastern end of the bridge from Perth Amboy to Staten Island.

The fare was fifty cents. Parker handed over two quarters, and went three-quarters of the way around the circle, then straight for about a hundred yards on cracked concrete, and took a right turn. This was 440, headed toward St. George, where the ferries docked.

The road was four lanes wide, made of concrete, with a center mall. But it looked abandoned. Old breaks had been lumpily covered with blacktop, and the more recent breaks had been ignored. Bushes and weeds grew wild on the mall, and the land to either side of the road was scrub.

"This is the way she'll come," he said to Handy, "After the job, she'll take the dirt road back of the diner, just the way she says. But she'll turn right instead of left, and come up just the way we did, up 9 and over 440 to the Outerbridge Crossing. She can take it easy along here, she's out of New Jersey."

Handy twisted around in the seat and looked behind them. "We're the only ones on the road."

"This route doesn't get much play. On a Monday, around noon, we'll have it all to ourselves."

"You're sure this is the way she'll come?"

"She's got to. It's the most direct way."

"What about those other two roads? Back there by the bridge, at the circle?"

Parker shrugged. "They don't go anywhere. This is the way to the ferry. There's what I want, up there."

He hit the brake, and the Ford slowed. At an angle off to the right was a cross street, or the beginning of a cross street. When this road was built, the curbs were put down with provisions for cross streets in the future, when Staten Island would be as big as Brooklyn.

The curb curved back on either side, and concrete started off to the right, going into the scrub about ten feet and stopping. Beyond was a gravel road for about a hundred feet, and beyond that a dirt road that curved back toward the main road but didn't come all the way. From 440, though, all you could see was the concrete starting out and then the gravel going off into the bushes.

Parker slowed the car, turned the wheel a little, and stopped just at the edge of the gravel. "Right here," he said. "The way I told you. We cut her off into this thing, take the dough, and go on to the ferry. Monday, around noon, we'll have ten or fifteen minutes before another car shows up. Besides, we're already in New York State."

They got out of the car. Handy tramped back and forth on the concrete, looking the situation over. He peered down at the gravel part, and stood there a minute, poking at his teeth with a wooden match. Then he shook his head and turned back.

"You know what bothers me?"

"What?"

"Skimm." Handy left the match in his mouth while he dug out a cigarette, talking around the match. "If he's on the outside and she figures to cross him, too, okay, then it'll work out like you say. But if she's sweet-talked him over, I don't like it. Skimm's no dummy. He'll try to think the way we think, and he'll come up with the idea they should stay away from Staten Island."

"Do you think he's in?"

Handy took time to light the cigarette and throw the match away. "I don't know. I've known Skimm twelve years. I've worked with him four, five times. I always figured Skimm was a little guy who didn't have much brains but you could trust him, you know what I mean?"

Parker nodded. "You think Alma wants him? After the job, I mean?"

"It doesn't figure."

"All she wants," said Parker, "is the money. Not half of it, all of it. She won't even try to sweet-talk Skimm."

"That's the way it plays," Handy answered. He looked around, at the empty road, and the gravel road that went nowhere. "We're taking a big chance on how it plays."

"She takes it out of Jersey for us, then we take it away from her. If the law stops her, that's one thing. If it doesn't, she'll come this way."

"It does figure," said Handy. His cigarette was all wet, where he'd lipped it. He stuck it back in his mouth. "All right, this is the way we do it."

"Right."

A pale blue Ford went by, headed toward the bridge to New Jersey. It was the first moving car they'd seen on Staten Island. They watched it go by, and then Parker said, "I got to get back. I got to walk Stubbs."

"You talk about him like he was your dog."

"He's a pain in the ass," Parker said.

They got into the car, made a U-turn at a break in the mall, and headed back to New Jersey.

3.

AFTER breakfast, Parker stopped at an outdoor phone booth next to a gas station. The Saturday morning traffic streaming by on 9 headed south for the shore. Parker dialed Skimm's number, and waited seven rings till there was a click and Skimm's voice said, "What?"

"It's ten o'clock," Parker said. Since Skimm had a woman, he'd been sleeping.

"What's that? Parker?"

"Yes."

"Listen, that guy called, that Lawson. He wants you to call him at his office, he'll be there till noon."

"All right. Walk Stubbs for me this afternoon, will you?"

"I was goin' to the shore with Alma." When Parker didn't say anything, Skimm said, "All right, I'll do it. That guy gives me a pain."

"I know," Parker said. "Hang around there while I talk to Lawson."

"Yeah, sure. I'll make some coffee. Alma's gone to work. She's gonna be mad when we can't go to the shore today."

"Yeah." Parker hung up, disgusted, and dropped another dime in the slot. He called Lawson's office, and an operator had him put in another fifteen. When he told the secretary it was Mr. Flynn to talk to Mr. Lawson she put him right through.

"I've got some of your goods, Mr. Flynn. Those three cases you wanted, in good condition, and one truck."

"Good," Parker said.

"The only thing is the truck right now is in North Caro-

59

lina. It's the one I told you about. It needs some work on it, but it'll run. They'll take eight hundred for delivery right there in North Carolina, no extras."

"How old is it?"

"Nine years."

Parker grimaced. "Will it make it up here?"

"According to what I've been told," Lawson said carefully, "it should make the trip, yes."

"All right. Where is it?"

"Goldsboro. I believe that's not too far from Raleigh."

"I'll find it. Who's the party?"

"The Double Ace Garage."

"All right."

"About the other matter, the three cases—"

"I'll pick them up Tuesday."

"Well," said Lawson, "I don't have them, but I can put you in touch with the man who does."

"Tell him Tuesday."

"I don't think he'll like that, Mr. Flynn. They're what you might call a perishable commodity. He doesn't like to keep them in the store too long, if you know what I mean."

"Tuesday's the earliest I can make it."

"Well, I tell you what. I'll give you his name and phone number. You can straighten it out with him."

"You straighten it out," Parker said. "I'll call you Tuesday."

He hung up and left the phone booth and joined the rest of the traffic on 9. Handy was sitting in Alma's green Dodge in the furniture store parking lot, across the road from the diner. Parker turned the Ford in next to him, and Handy came over, sliding in next to Parker in the Ford. He had a pencil and a notebook with him.

"What's the good word?" he said.

"I got to go to North Carolina to pick up a truck. I'll

try to be back Monday. Walk Stubbs for me tomorrow, will you?"

"Sure. Skimm taking it today?"

"Yeah."

"He's supposed to take over here for me tomorrow morning."

"I know."

"What kind of truck you—*There* he goes!" He pointed the pencil at the road. "See him? The light green Merc with the white top. He's either law or on a case."

Parker squinted at the Mercury as it faded away down the road, southward. "Law, I guess. Shows up when the traffic's heavy?"

"Right. The same two guys in it every time." Handy made a mark in the notebook. "I don't think he'll be working Monday, but just the same." He looked out at the road again. "What kind of truck you got?"

"I don't know. A bomb, I think."

"Just so it's big."

"You can use the Ford while I'm gone. I'll leave it with Skimm."

Handy nodded. "I'll see you Monday."

"If the truck doesn't break down."

"If you don't show, I'll take care of Stubbs."

"Right."

Handy went back to his own car and Parker drove north into Irvington and stopped at Skimm's house. Skimm was dressed but he hadn't shaved. His beard grew in straggly and gray, making him look more like a wino on the bum. "Come on in, I'm making coffee," he said.

Skimm went back to the kitchen and Parker called Newark Airport. He could get a plane at two-fifty, change over in Washington and go from there to Raleigh. After that he'd take a bus to Goldsboro. He made the reservation, and then went out to the kitchen.

Skimm was standing by the stove, watching a battered

tin coffee pot. He'd spent so much of his life jungled up he didn't know how to make coffee any other way but in an old beat-up pot. There were two heavy china mugs on the table, and steel spoons, but no saucers. A pint of Old Mr. Boston stood next to one mug.

"Sit down," Skimm said, "she's almost ready."

Parker sat down at the table and lit a cigarette. "You got an ash tray?"

"Yeah, wait a second." Skimm looked around and then brought a saucer over to the table. "Here you are."

"Thanks." Parker dropped the match onto the saucer.

Skimm went back over to the stove and watched the coffee pot some more. Over his shoulder, he said, "Things comin' along, huh?"

"Yeah."

"I guess you were right, Parker. We only needed three men. Even with that Stubbs to louse things up."

"You want to watch him this afternoon. Yesterday, he started to throw a two-by-four at me."

Skimm bobbed his head and grinned. "Getting stir-crazy, huh?"

"Just another week," Parker said. He shrugged. "I'm going south today, be back Monday. Picking up a truck. Come out to the airport with me and take the car. Use it when you go walk Stubbs and then let Handy have it."

"Okay." Skimm turned the fire off under the coffee pot and poured them two cups of coffee. He set out milk and sugar for Parker, and poured a belt of Old Mr. Boston in with his coffee. Then he sat down. "You got a truck, huh?"

Parker nodded.

"A good one?"

"How do I know till I see it?"

"That's right, ain't it?" Skimm sipped at his coffee, and made a face. "You say it's down south?"

"North Carolina."

"North Carolina," repeated Skimm. "And you going to fly down, huh?"

"Shut up a while," Parker said.

Skimm blinked rapidly for a few seconds, and then looked down at his coffee cup. He took another sip, and made a face again. Then he coughed, and looked slant-eyed at Parker. Parker just sat there, smoking a cigarette and drinking coffee, waiting for it to be time to go to the airport.

After a while, Skimm coughed again. "You getting nervous about it, Parker?"

Parker focused on him slowly. He'd been miles away. "Nervous about what?"

"You know. The job."

"No."

"I thought—you acted jumpy."

"Irritated," Parker answered. "The job isn't clean, there's too much to watch."

"You mean Stubbs?"

Parker shrugged.

"Listen," Skimm said. "I know you don't like Alma. She's kind of bitchy sometimes, I know that. But she's okay, Parker, she really is. You got to get to know her. I wish you'd try to get to know her."

Parker looked at him, his mouth dragging down at the corners. "You offering her to me?"

Skimm got confused then, and looked at his coffee cup. "No, no, I didn't mean that, nothing like that. I only meant—" He ran down, not sure how to explain himself.

"Sure," said Parker. He finished his coffee and got to his feet. "Let's go out to the airport."

"What time's your plane?"

"Two-fifty."

"We got time, then."

"I want to go now."

"Sure. Okay." Skimm stood up and finished his coffee,

gulping it down. He started to put the pint in his pocket, but Parker said, "Leave it. You're going to be driving."

"Okay. Sure."

They went out to the car, and Parker drove to the airport. When he got out of the car, he said, "You let Stubbs get away, I'll stomp you!"

"Don't you worry," said Skimm. "He won't go nowhere."

Parker walked away into the terminal.

4.

GOLDSBORO is small and pinch-faced, a backwater town on the Neuse River, surrounded by tobacco fields. There's an air base nearby, and the State Hospital for Negro Insane. These, and cotton and fertilizer, are what the town lives on.

Parker got off the bus a little after ten, Saturday night. The workers and the airmen filled the streets. He pushed through and went into a diner where he got directions to the Double Ace Garage. It was too far to walk, so he went back to the tiny bus depot and took the only cab, an old black Chevrolet.

The Double Ace Garage was a long, low, shed-like construction of concrete blocks. It was painted a dirty white, with the name in red lettering over the wide doors at the front. Parker went inside to the office cubicle, stuck in the right hand corner up front, and found a hairy florid stout man sitting in a swivel chair at a rolltop desk. He was smoking a cigar, and he left it in his mouth when he talked.

"I'm Flynn. Lawson sent me."

"Yah," said the florid man. He turned slightly, and the swivel chair squeaked drily. "He phoned."

"Let's see it," Parker said.

"Yah. You're in a hurry, hah?"

Parker waited.

The florid man grunted and heaved himself out of the chair. They went around to the side of the building, where there was a gravel lot. The truck was standing there, a nine-year-old Dodge cab and a Fruehauf trailer, lit by a floodlight on the side of the building. The trailer was metal color and covered with grime, and the cab red. Some company name on the doors had been painted out with a darker red. The engine was running.

Parker shook his head. He went over and opened the door on the driver's side and reached up and turned the ignition key. The engine stopped. The florid man watched him, chewing slowly on his cigar, but Parker ignored him. He looked at the rubber all the way around. It was all lousy but at least there were no threads showing.

The mudguards were gone, and so were most of the safety lights. The window was broken in the righthand door, and there was some sort of jury-rigged rope arrangement keeping cab and trailer together because the original hitch was broken. The floor mats were gone in the cab, showing where part of the metal flooring had rusted through.

Parker opened the trailer doors and saw that most of the wooden inner walls had been ripped out. He shook his head again and went around front to open the left side of the hood. The engine was a greasy mess, the wiring frayed, the radiator hoses cracked. The dip stick was gone, and so was the breather.

Parker closed the hood again, got down, and wiped his hands on the fender. Then he crawled under the cab.

There was a large oil stain on the ground, and the lube points were practically covered by caked-on dirt.

He came out from under the cab. "She's a mess."

The florid man grinned around his cigar, and spread his hands. "For the price?" he said. "Come on back to the office."

Parker went with him back to the office. The florid man started to say, "I know she don't look—" when Parker turned around and went back out again. The florid man looked startled. "Hey! Where you goin'?"

Parker went around to the side of the building again. A kid in a greasy coverall had the hood open. There was a battery on the ground beside the cab, and he was getting set to attach the jumper cables.

The florid man came heavily around the corner. "Now, listen here, buddy."

Parker turned to him. "I want a new battery," he said. "And new plugs. And fresh oil. And a lube. And enough lights on the box so I don't get stopped by state troopers."

The florid man was shaking his head, chewing more rapidly on the cigar. "That wasn't the deal. As is, that was the deal, as is."

"No deal," Parker said. He walked around the florid man and started toward the street.

"Hey, wait a minute!"

Parker turned.

The florid man tried a smile that didn't come off. "No sense goin' off in a huff, buddy," he said. "We can work somethin' out. It might maybe cost you a little more, but just for the parts, not for the labor. I wouldn't charge you for the labor."

"Do like I said with it," Parker answered, "and new radiator hoses, and I'll take it for seven."

"Seven! The deal was eight."

"It isn't worth eight. It'll never be worth eight."

"Now, buddy," the florid man said, "you got a chip

on your shoulder. Now, why don't we just talk this over? Come on back to the office."

"Tell your boy to put a new battery in."

The florid man tried another smile. This one worked better. "Not a *new* battery, buddy, I wouldn't try to snow you. But a better one than you got. Okay?"

"Good."

"There you go. You see, we can get along." He turned and shouted, "Hey, Willis! Never mind about that. Take that old battery out of there, and put that Delta in. You know the one."

"And leave the engine off," added Parker.

"Yeah, sure, buddy. Leave her off, Willis."

Willis gathered up his battery and jumper cables and went back through the side door into the garage again.

Parker and the florid man went back to the office, and this time Parker sat down in the slat-bottomed wooden chair beside the desk. The florid man settled heavily into the swivel chair, making it squeal. "I can see you know about trucks, buddy."

"I thought you wouldn't snow me," Parker said.

"Now, there's that chip on your shoulder again." He made a little tsk-tsk sound, and shook his head in a friendly sort of way. Then he pulled an order-blank pad and a pencil over. "Now, then. What else did you want?"

"Lube. Oil change. New plugs. Check the points. New—"

"Points? Now, you keep adding something every single time."

"Are you writing all this down?"

"I surely am." The florid man wrote "points," and asked, "What else?"

"New radiator hoses. And the legal minimum of lights."

The florid man wrote, laboriously, chewing on his cigar. The cigar had gone out, but he kept chewing on it anyway. When he was done writing, he said, "Now, let's see.

Lube and oil change, I guess I can do that all right. And plugs, well, we can check 'em out, clean 'em up a little. But I don't see any way we could give you *new* ones."

"New ones," Parker said.

"Now, buddy." The florid man spread his arms. "I give a little, you give a little."

"Tell me about that Delta," Parker said. "The one you're giving me."

The florid man cocked his head and sucked on the cold cigar. Then he smiled again. "New plugs. I just might be able to do it."

"That's fine."

"Okay, now, let's see what else we got. The points. Well, sure, that's no problem. And those hoses." He nodded slowly, the cigar moving around in his mouth. "I noticed them myself, but I don't think I got hoses like that in stock. I tell you what I'll do, though. I'll have Willis tape them up solid with friction tape. What do you say? You won't leak a drop."

"There's an oil leak, too."

"Now, there you go adding things again."

"The breather's gone."

"I *know* I don't have that in stock."

"Cap it, then. I don't want to keep throwing oil away."

"Cap it? I can cap it, right enough. It's just I don't have that in stock." He looked down at the list again. "Now, this about the lights. There sure are a lot of lights on there now."

"Not enough. There have to be lights at all outer corners, top and bottom, front and back of the box."

"I'm not sure the wiring's there any more."

"It won't take much to wire. You don't have to be neat about it."

"Well, I'll see what I can do." The florid man looked· at the list, studying it. "I do believe I can take care of all this for you, and still only ask the original price of eight hundred."

"We'll see what kind of a job you do."

"Don't you worry, my friend," the florid man said. "I'll take care of you right. You just leave everything to me."

"One more thing."

The florid man looked up, frowning.

"I saw Alabama plates on her. Are they hot?"

"Not where you're going, way up in New Jersey."

"What about when I drive through North Carolina?"

"I tell you what I'll do. I'll smear some mud on 'em, so you can't tell the difference." He took the cigar out of his mouth at last. "You know, safe plates are expensive. I got some, safe as a mother's arms, but I just wouldn't let them get tossed in on this deal. Safe plates aren't that easy to come by."

"All right. Smear mud on them."

"That's just what I'll do." He tore the top sheet off the order blank pad. "Now, when do you want to take her? Tomorrow morning?"

"Tonight."

"Oh, you want a *rush* job."

"I want her tonight," Parker said. "And don't give me a lot of crap about that being extra."

"Why, I had no intention. I tell you what, friend, you come back here at midnight—that's two hours from now or a little less—and she'll be ready."

"That's good," Parker said.

He left the office. A block away he found a hole-in-the-wall restaurant and spent some time over a cup of coffee. Then he walked around a while, looking at the town, glad he was going to be leaving it that night. At midnight he walked back to the Double Ace Garage.

The truck was out on the side again, but in a different spot, closer to the floodlight. Parker went over and looked at it. There were new spark plugs, the joints had been lubed, the breather hole was capped, and lights had been haphazardly attached to the trailer. Friction tape had been wrapped tightly around the radiator hoses and mud had been smeared on the Alabama plates. And the stain on the ground under the cab came from cleaner oil.

Parker swung up into the cab and turned the key in the ignition. She started sluggishly, but she started. The engine roared, and the cab trembled. There was either no muffler or it was riddled with holes.

Parker saw the florid man coming toward him across the gravel. He had a new cigar now, lit. He stopped beside the cab and shouted up over the roar of the engine, "How do you like her?"

"Get in," Parker shouted back. "Let's go around the block."

The florid man hesitated. "Hold on just a second."

He went back toward the office. When he came back, he had a jacket on, with a bulging righthand pocket. He climbed into the cab, and Parker fought into second.

The mirror on the left was cracked, and the mirror on the right was gone. Using just the one on the left, Parker backed till he was facing the driveway to the street, and then drove out. The trailer was long and high. Because it was empty, and because of the bad way it was attached to the cab, it tracked badly as Parker made the wide turn onto the street.

The brakes were better than Parker had expected, though he had to pump them up a little each time. But the acceleration was lousy and the cab seemed ready to shake itself apart any second. They went around the block, having trouble on all the turns because of the way the trailer tracked, and when they got to the garage again Parker left the truck in the street. "All right," he said. "Eight hundred."

"She's old," the florid man answered, petting the grimy dashboard, "but she's rugged. She'll get you there."

"Lawson's already got his piece," Parker said, "so you get seven-twenty." He had it ready, in an envelope in his coat pocket.

He handed it over, and the florid man counted the money, slowly, his lips moving as his blunt fingers shuffled the bills. There were six twenties, and these he held out over the dashboard where the light from the street light would hit them. "There's been some trouble with twenties lately."

"I'm not in that business," Parker said.

"It always pays to be careful." The florid man finished inspecting the bills. "That's fine. Well, you're all set now. You got yourself a good buy."

He opened the door and clambered down to the street. He slammed the door and waved, and went on into the garage, stuffing the bills back into the envelope. Parker fought the gearshift into second again, and started off.

He took 117 north out of Goldsboro and picked up 301 the other side of Fremont, then 301 north into Virginia. The friction tape on the hoses hadn't been enough. The radiator itself leaked. Parker had to make his first stop at Richmond, after going one hundred and seventy miles. He had the radiator filled, and a can of sealant added. They checked the oil, and he needed a quart already.

The other side of Richmond, he stayed on 301 to bypass Washington and Baltimore. He crossed Chesapeake Bay, kept on 301 across the state line into Delaware, and had to stop short of Wilmington because the radiator had run dry again. The truck also took another quart of oil.

He'd now done three hundred and fifty some miles, and it was ten o'clock in the morning. The steady hard jouncing in the cab and the number of hours he'd gone without sleep caught up with him, and he pulled into a motel south of Wilmington. He didn't start again until eleven o'clock that night. It was better to drive at night anyway, less like-lihood of being stopped by the law.

After Wilmington, he crossed into Pennsylvania for a while, on 202, bypassing Philadelphia, then crossed into New Jersey at New Hope. He passed through Flemington at three in the morning, and just the other side of there the oil gauge told him he had trouble. He pushed fifteen miles to Somerville, but couldn't find a gas station open, so he kept going, switching to 22, and picking up 18, to limp into New Brunswick.

He found a good-sized garage open, but they had no mechanic on duty Sunday night. He'd come on at seven o'clock, so Parker left the truck there and went away to get something to eat. He was glad to be out of the cab for a while. It had bucked and tossed him for five hundred miles, and he was a little surprised it had made it this far.

After eating, he went back and talked with the nightman at the garage. The pumps were all lit up out on the tarmac, but at five o'clock on a Monday morning there were no customers. After a while the nightman took a nap and Parker sat in the office, smoking and looking out at the truck. It was a bad truck, but it had done better than he'd expected. So maybe the job wouldn't go completely sour after all, despite Alma and Stubbs and the bored state trooper.

When the mechanic came in at seven o'clock he looked at the truck in disgust. He got interested, though, being a professional, and worked on it till nine-thirty. By then, the boss was in, and he charged Parker thirty-seven dollars.

Parker asked for a receipt, and thanked the mechanic. The mechanic told him he had maybe five hundred miles left in the truck, and where he should drive was straight to a dealer for a trade-in, while it could still make it under its own power. "The way I got it fixed," he said, "a dealer might think it was worth taking in and doing some work on."

Parker gave him five for himself and told him he'd probably be back with the truck some time. Then he left New Brunswick on route 1, took it north to where it met 9, and turned south.

He got to the Shore Points Diner at ten after ten and pulled in to the side lot, just to the left of where the armored car usually stopped. He climbed down from the cab and went across the highway to the furniture store parking lot. Handy was there, in the Ford. Parker slipped in beside him. "That's it. Over there. Cost me thirty-seven bucks in New Brunswick to keep it going."

"That's a real nice scow," Handy said.

"Take it up to Newark and stash it on a side street tonight."

"Right."

Parker handed over the ignition key. "And take some paint and fix up the doors, will you? Put some kind of brand name on them."

"Will do." Handy looked down to the right. "Here she comes."

They watched the red armored car come down the highway, slow, and turn at the diner. It rolled up the blacktop to the gravel at the side and slid into its usual parking slot. Parker and Handy watched it disappear behind the truck, and Handy grinned. "Right out of sight."

Parker nodded. "The job's going to work out."

5.

THE man who had the guns was named Fox. *Maurice Fox,* it said on the window of the store, *Plumbing Equipment.* Inside, the store was long and narrow and dark. There were dusty toilets in one row, porcelain sinks in another row, and bins full of pipe joints and faucets along one wall.

A short balding man in a rumpled gray suit and bent glasses came down the aisle between the rows of toilets and sinks. "Yes?"

"I'm Flynn. You've got three pipes for me."

"Yes. I didn't like holding them so long." He blinked steadily behind the glasses, and his eyes looked watery. "All the way from Thursday, and now Tuesday already."

"I couldn't make it before."

"It's bad business." He shook his head, eyes still blinking steadily. "Come along."

He turned and led the way down the aisle, Parker behind him. They went through a doorway to the back and down a flight of stairs with just steps and no risers to a plaster-walled basement. Fox clicked a light switch on a beam, and to the left a bare bulb came on.

Fox led the way to a wooden partition with a heavy wooden door. He took a ring full of keys from his pocket, selected the one he wanted, and unlocked the door. They went inside, and Fox lit another bare bulb. He closed the door after Parker.

The room was small and made smaller by the cases lining it on all four sides. The floor was wooden slats over concrete, except for one square in the middle, where there was no wood over the drain. Along the back wall the crates were on shelves, and Fox went over to them and reached into one of the crates and took out a Sauer 7.65-mm. automatic. He handed this to Parker, reached in again, and brought out a Police Positive .38 revolver. On the third dip, he came up with a short-barreled Smith & Wesson .32 revolver.

Parker looked them over. The Sauer still had its serial number, but it had been filed off the other two. He looked closer at the .32 and saw that acid had been used, after the filing.

Fox rummaged in another crate, and came up with two small boxes marked "Nails." One also had an X on it. "The one with the X is .32 calibre. The other one is .38."

"All right."

For the last time, Fox felt around in one of the crates, and this time he brought out two clips for the Sauer. "You'll want to check them?"

"Right."

Fox went to the middle of the room, got down on his knees, and lifted up the drain plate. Underneath was loose dirt. "In here," he said, getting to his feet again. "Don't worry about the sound. The boxes keep it all in. It will be very loud, because the room's so small, but outside no one will hear a thing."

Parker put the two revolvers and the boxes of ammunition on top of a closed wooden crate, and slipped one of the clips into the Sauer. He stood wide-legged and aimed straight down into the drain. He switched the safety off, and fired. There was a tremendous noise, ricocheting off the walls and cases. Parker clicked the safety back on, removed the clip, and sighted through the barrel at the light bulb. The gun was in good condition.

Fox put one bullet in the cylinder of the .32 and another in the cylinder of the .38, and Parker tried them both. When he had finished, his ears were ringing. The

.32 was in somewhat ragged shape—he nicked concrete at the edge of the hole when he fired it—but usable, and the other two were fine. He nodded. "How much?"

Fox pointed at the three guns lying on the crate. "Seventy-five and seventy-five and sixty. Two hundred and ten. And including the ammunition."

"The .32 isn't very good. It isn't worth sixty."

Fox shrugged. "Fifty, then. Two hundred even."

"All right."

Parker counted out the money, and Fox stowed it away in an old wallet. Then he carefully packed the three guns and the ammunition in a small wooden box with excelsior padding around them, and tacked the lid on tight. "You should clean them when you get home."

"I will."

They went back upstairs, and Parker went out the front door and got into the Ford. He drove to Irvington and left the guns with Skimm to clean and hide. Then he went down to the farmhouse to walk Stubbs.

6.

THEY got the other truck that Thursday, from Harrisburg, Pennsylvania. Handy went for it, because that was the day Parker fixed up a license for himself and a registration. It was a printer he went to, and once again the contact was through Lawson. It took three hours, and then Parker went to the body shop to wait for Handy and the truck.

The body shop was in Dover, and the owner, a sullen man in an undershirt, had heard from Lawson that Parker would be coming. Parker introduced himself as Flynn, and then waited around for Handy.

Handy got there at seven-thirty that evening. The truck was six years old. The cab was a wide International Harvester, painted green, and the trailer another Fruehauf. This one had cost more—fifteen hundred—and was a much better truck. It had been stripped of heater and mudguards and floor mats and all but the legal minimum of lights, but at least it was in sound running condition and the trailer was in good shape. The original plates had been Pennsylvania and as hot as it was possible to get, so Handy had had to pay a hundred extra for safe plates from Indiana.

Parker studied the trailer, and it would work out fine. There were two rear doors plus one door on each side at the midpoint. The wooden inner shell was scuffed up but intact. Parker told the body shop owner what he wanted —the rear doors and the right side door sealed permanently, and a lock on the outside of the left side door which would be guaranteed to keep people in. He and Handy went off to a diner and had coffee and then to a movie.

When they came back, just before midnight, the job was done. The owner wanted a hundred, but they gave him eighty. The bankroll was getting low, less than five hundred left.

They drove to Newark, and Handy left the truck in a street already lined with trucks. Then he and Parker drove to where they'd parked the other truck yesterday, and Handy drove it eight blocks away and parked it again. It wasn't good to leave a vehicle in one spot more than twenty-four hours. After they moved the second truck, they drove down to the Shore Points Diner.

It was now nearly four o'clock, Friday morning. The diner was closed and there was practically no traffic on route 9. Handy kept the watch in his hand, looking at it by the dash light, and Parker gunned out of the lot.

He had to go south first, make a U-turn, and then go north again. There were only two traffic lights along this stretch of 9, and they slowed when they reached the first one, to be sure they caught it red.

When it changed, Parker jumped to fifty and they flew past the second one. He had to slow to make the turn to 440, where there was a looping circle that went away to the right after 9 passed under 440. The turnoff came up a rise and stopped at 440, and you could make either a right or a left. There was a stop sign, and they would have to make a left.

They stopped, though there was no traffic, and Handy counted slowly to ten, looking at the watch in his hand. Then Parker made the left and they coasted at forty-five, the speed limit here, to the next light. They reached it just before it turned green, and had to come to a complete stop.

"Fifteen next time," Handy said.

"Right."

Next, there came a circle, and then another light, which turned red when they were about fifty yards away.

"This one's going to be a bitch," Handy said.

"I'll be going through the other one faster," Parker said. "I'll hit it a little heavier coming around the circle. Thirty instead of twenty-five."

"It'll be daytime. There'll be traffic."

"It's a bitch doing it this way," Parker said.

Ordinarily, they would have made this dry run on a Monday morning at eleven o'clock, but either Alma or Skimm would have seen them at it and wondered what they were doing.

When the light changed, Parker drove on down to the bridge but didn't bother to go across. There were no more lights from here to the turnoff. He circled around and went back to the diner, once again making sure he was stopped by the first light. When it changed to green, he pulled away and was making fifty by the time they passed the diner.

"Seventeen seconds," Handy said.

"All right."

They went around again, waited for the light to turn red before coming back down. Parker tore into the gravel parking lot, squealing the brakes at the last second, and swung around in the position they'd be in during the job.

"Thirteen," Handy said. "Fourteen. Fifteen. Sixteen. Seventeen."

Parker made the trip again, out of the diner, south to the U-turn, then north. They went through the first light and Handy looked back at it, counting. It changed ten seconds after they went by. They went through the middle of the second light, made the turn to 440, and Handy counted to ten again, because the timing was different now. They went through the first light just after it went green, and the second one just before it went red.

"That's all right, now," Parker said.

"If the lights work the same in the daytime."

"They might change them at rush hour. Not at eleven in the morning."

"Still—"

"I'll try it once more tomorrow morning, just to be sure."

Parker drove Handy back to his place in Newark, then turned around and went back to his motel. He wrote a note asking to be called at ten o'clock, and dropped it through the mail slot in the office door. It seemed as if he was barely asleep when the woman who ran the motel was knocking at the door.

He got up and showered and ate breakfast and drove to the diner. Skimm was stationed in the furniture store parking lot and he went over and talked to him for a few minutes, leaving the Ford parked beside the diner. Then he went back over to the Ford, backing out of the parking space so he was in the position he'd be in during the job.

He paused to light a cigarette, watching the road. Traffic went by, headed south, and as the leader went by, Parker pulled out of the lot and fell in behind him. He went over the course again, and the lights worked the same in the daytime.

Satisfied, he went to the farmhouse and let Stubbs out in the air for two hours. Stubbs was surly and nervous. He'd refused to talk for the last two days, and he still refused to talk. The tic in his left check that had started yesterday was worse.

7.

SATURDAY, Handy went shopping around in different stores and pieced together a dark blue guard's uniform. That afternoon, to keep Skimm and Alma happy, they all got together and made a timed dry run of the getaway.

Alma and Skimm jumped into the Dodge and went bumping off into the scrub back of the diner, and Parker and Handy pushed the Ford south on 9. They were to go south on 9, turn right on 516 to 18 and then left on Main Street and on to the farmhouse. Alma and Skimm were coming around the back way, down the Amboy Turnpike. That's the way it was being done today, with everybody playing games and being serious about it, and Skimm the only one who thought it was for real.

When Parker and Handy got to the dirt road turnoff to the farmhouse, the green Dodge was already there, parked on the shoulder of the road. Parker stopped behind it and kept his motor running. He didn't like the two cars together like this, so close to the time of the job.

Skimm came over from the Dodge and leaned in the window. "How'd it go?"

"Sweet," Handy said. "No problems."

"We ought to run through it again," Skimm said.

Parker shook his head. He was disgusted because he had to play a part when he should be concentrating on the job.

"Alma doesn't want to either," Skimm said.

"She's right." Handy answered.

"We'll go into the farmhouse," Parker said.

Skimm went back to the Dodge, and Parker turned the Ford across the road and went up the dirt track and around the tree and down to the farmhouse. He parked in back, and he and Handy got out and stretched. Then Parker went inside and took the automatic from the card table and unbarred the door. He kicked the door and stepped back. "Come on out."

Stubbs came out. He didn't have anything in his hands, and he wasn't watching for a chance to jump Parker. He'd stopped all that four or five days ago, around the same time he'd stopped shaving.

Parker had brought him shaving gear the third day, and for a while Stubbs had shaved every day or so, but now he'd stopped. His beard was spiny, dark brown flecked with gray. His mouth looked dirty too, with spittle caked white on the lips, and he kept his eyes half-closed against the light.

When Parker told him to go on outside in the air, he shuffled, keeping his arms at his sides. His movements were getting shorter and more economical every day.

When Stubbs and Parker came out, Alma and Skimms were standing with Handy, talking. Stubbs stopped and looked at them, blinking some more. He'd been at the farmhouse twelve days now, and this was the first he'd seen more than one person at a time.

Parker held the automatic loose at his side. "Walk around," he said, "but don't go near the cars."

Stubbs walked around, in a large ragged circle. His shuffling made the white sand kick up around his feet. His shoes and pantcuffs were covered with sand, and his white shirt was almost gray. He'd stopped wearing the chauffeur's jacket and cap, and his squat head looked naked, as though his hair was getting thinner. He shuffled around in a circle, head bowed and eyes looking at the ground, while the other four stood by the farmhouse and talked.

They went over the job, what each of them was supposed to do and how long it would take. Who was supposed to be where when. Parker went over it, and then each of the others went over his part of it, explaining it as though the other three didn't know anything about it. There were questions, mostly from Alma and mostly useless because they weren't about Alma's part of it, but the questions were all answered.

Stubbs interrupted after a while, shuffling over and telling Parker he had to go out around to the other side of the farmhouse because of the woman. Parker went with him, and while he waited he listened to the drone of the three voices from around back.

Shortly afterward, they finished and everybody seemed satisfied. Alma and Skimm got back into the Dodge, and drove around the farmhouse and back up toward the road. Handy and Parker stayed a while longer, so Stubbs could have more time out in the air. It looked to Parker as though Stubbs might be getting sick, since he wasn't shaving or trying to fight back any more. He wanted Stubbs to stay healthy.

Handy said to Stubbs, "It's almost over, partner. By Monday night, you'll be away from here."

"It's always night," said Stubbs. It was almost the first thing he'd said, and his voice was low and flat, as though he didn't care if anybody heard him.

Handy felt sorry for Stubbs. He'd been inside, and he knew this must be even worse than inside, because of being alone and no light. "Listen, there's a flashlight in the car. Why don't we give you the flashlight?"

"For what?" Parker said.

Handy shrugged. "To break the monotony."

Parker looked at Stubbs. It wasn't easy keeping a man on ice, not for anybody concerned. But Stubbs had bulled in, complicating things. Parker's concern for him was really limited—keep him healthy, and keep him on ice, until after the job; then go with him to Nebraska and square things with the cook, May. Then it was over. He didn't have any interest in Stubbs other than that, so he'd never thought about giving him a flashlight.

Handy got the flashlight out of the glove compartment of the Ford and brought it over to Stubbs. Stubbs took it as though it was a piece of wood, and just let it dangle in his hand at the end of his arm. Then he went off and shuffled around in his circle again, holding onto the flashlight. Just before they put him back in he tried the flashlight and it worked. He looked at the circle of light on the ground and smiled. Then he went back inside and Parker barred the door.

8.

You don't do anything the day before a job. You just lie around and take it easy. Parker went to a movie in the afternoon and another in the evening, then had some beer in a bar. He wanted to take a six pack back to the motel, but in New Jersey you can't buy a six pack after ten o'clock at night.

He was up at seven Monday morning and drove up to Irvington to Skimm's place. Skimm had the Dodge. He gave Parker the Sauer and the .38, keeping the .32 for himself, and they took the two cars to Newark and picked up Handy. Handy rode with Parker, and Parker gave him the .38.

They picked up the good truck, and Handy drove that. All three of them went back to the Shore Points Diner, where Alma was already at work. The parking lot on the side they wanted was empty. They put the Ford in the spot where the armored car always parked, and the good truck to the right of it, on the side away from the road. Handy went into the diner, and Parker and Skimm went back up to Newark again in the Dodge.

They got the other truck, the bad one, and Parker drove it down 9 to the other side of the Raritan River and then parked on the shoulder and took out a roadmap. He sat studying the roadmap. Skimm stopped a little farther south, at the bottom of a long curving grade, where he could see a long way back. He also spent some time studying a roadmap. It was five minutes to ten.

They were all in position now. The good truck was where it would be during the job. The Ford was next to it, parked at an angle so it blocked where the armored car would be and where the bad truck would be, so no other customers could take those places. Skimm and Parker were two miles north, waiting for the armored car. Handy was in the diner, having a cup of coffee.

At ten after ten, Alma told Benjy to mop up the right side. She put a chair across the aisle and a cardboard sign on it saying, "Section closed." There was one couple in a booth on that side, but they left at quarter after ten, when the ammonia from Benjy's mop got to them. Handy

left right after them, and sat in the Ford, taking a while
to get a cigarette lit.

At twenty-five past ten, Skimm saw the armored car
top the rise way behind him. He started the Dodge, pulled
out onto the highway and drove south at the speed limit,
fifty miles an hour. When Handy saw him go by, he backed
the Ford away from the diner and drove south after him.
As soon as the armored car passed Parker he put the roadmap away, fought the gearshift into second, and followed.
Skimm, south of the diner, took the first U-turn and came
back north again. Handy went on to the second U-turn
and then came back.

The armored car pulled in to the diner and stopped in
its normal place, next to the good truck. The driver got
out and went to the back and let the guard out. They
locked that door and went into the diner. As they were
going through the door, Parker showed up in the bad truck
and slid it into the slot to the left of the armored car. He
got down from the cab and went into the diner. He sat
on the stool nearest the cash register, and ordered coffee.

Skimm came north again, passing the diner to make
sure the bad truck blotted out the view of the armored
car, and kept going north. At the junction with 35 he did
the loop-the-loop and wound up going south again. He
stopped just shy of the entrance to the diner parking lot,
and got out his roadmap. He left the engine running.

Handy came north, took the first crossover, went by
Skimm in the Dodge, and drove around behind the diner.
He already had the blue pants on, and now he changed
to the blue shirt and put on a tie. He strapped on the belt
and holster and slid the .38 in the holster. He put on the
sunglasses, but held the garrison cap in his hand.

Inside the diner, Parker saw the driver and the guard
getting ready to leave. He was at the register already, so
he paid before they did, and went outside. When they
came out, they saw him kicking at the right front tire of

the cab, standing between the cab and the armored car. Then he walked back and looked at the double rear tires of the cab on the same side, and shook his head. When the driver and the guard were almost to him, he moved again, and studied the double tires at the back of the trailer. He shook his head angrily and said, "I'll be a son of a bitch."

He said it loud, and the driver and the guard looked at him and grinned.

When they had disappeared from Skimm's sight behind the bad truck, he had put the roadmap down and shifted the Dodge into first. He drove slowly into the parking lot and stopped facing the woods behind the diner, his left front fender next to the rear of the good truck and his left rear fender next to the rear of the bad truck.

When Handy heard Parker say, "I'll be a son of a bitch," he put his garrison cap on and walked around the side of the diner toward the good truck.

The driver took out a key and turned it in the back door of the armored car. Then he stepped back and the guard took out another key and finished the job of unlocking the door. He pulled the door open as Parker came walking forward, and when he started up into the back of the armored car Parker clipped him with the butt of the Sauer.

Just then Handy came around the back of the good truck, with the .38 in his right hand and a small pocket-knife in his left. He put the point of the gun in the driver's back and pricked the side of his neck with the knife.

"Hold very still," he said, low and flat. The gun was the real threat, but the knife was psychological. Most people were more afraid of a knife than a gun.

The driver shivered, and his eyes widened. Parker said to him, talking low, "Go on up and have the other guard open the door for you."

Handy moved his left hand down and pricked the

knife gently into the driver's hip. "One wrong move," he said, "and I castrate you."

Skimm got out of the Dodge, bringing the rope and gags. He and Parker tied and gagged the unconscious guard, and carried him to the side of the good truck. Parker opened the door, and they tossed the guard inside. Then he went around to the other side of the armored car to help Handy.

The guard in the cab of the armored car saw the driver, and caught a glimpse of another uniformed figure behind him. He opened the door on the driver's side, and saw a flash of reflected light as the driver went down. Then Handy had the .38 on him. "Come on out!"

The guard hesitated. He could see the driver lying on his face on the gravel. He swallowed, and came carefully out of the armored car.

Parker sapped him as he stepped down. He and Skimm tied and gagged the driver and the second guard, while Handy started moving the sacks and boxes from the armored car to the Dodge. Parker and Skimm tossed the trussed two into the good truck with the first guard, and then Parker locked the door while Skimm went to help Handy. When the door was locked, Parker helped finish the transfer from the armored car to the Dodge.

Inside the diner, Alma walked across Benjy's wet floor while Benjy glared at her, and looked out the window. She saw they were finishing, so she went through the kitchen and out the back door, slipping a paring knife into her purse.

Skimm got behind the wheel of the Dodge, and Parker and Handy walked back around to the Ford. The job had taken three minutes. Alma came out as Handy was changing his shirt, and said, "See you at the farmhouse."

"Right," said Handy. Parker was behind the wheel of the Ford and didn't say anything.

The Dodge came around the corner of the building, its rear end low because of the weight in it now, and stopped. Skimm slid over, and Alma got behind the wheel. The Dodge shot off along the dirt road.

Handy finished changing his shirt and came around to get into the Ford on the passenger's side. He tossed the blue shirt and the belt and holster and the garrison cap on the floor behind the front seat. Parker started the Ford and they went around the diner and paused near the two trucks and the armored car.

Traffic went by, headed south, and then there was no traffic. When the traffic started again, Parker joined it and they went over the course with no trouble, catching all the lights. They went across the bridge and paid the fifty cent toll at the Mission-style toll booth and went around the circle to 440. They felt easier now, because they were in a different state, but Parker still drove fast. There was a car far ahead of them, nothing behind them. One car went by in the other direction, toward the bridge.

When they got to the spot they'd chosen for the trap, Parker turned left through the gap in the mall. He shifted into neutral, put on the emergency brake, and got out of the car. In the trunk were sunglasses and a red baseball cap and a red flag and a large metal sign that said, "Detour," in black letters on a yellow background.

Parker put on the sunglasses and the baseball cap, and stuck the red flag in his back pocket. He looked both ways, but there was no traffic, so he crossed the road and found a dead branch on the other side. He used that to prop up the detour sign in the righthand lane, just beyond the dead-end turnoff. In the meantime, Handy turned the Ford around so it was backed into the bushes and facing across the road. When Alma took the detour, he'd drive across and block her exit.

Parker lit a cigarette and waited. A pale green Volkswagen came along, and slowed when it saw Parker and the detour sign. Parker took out the red flag and motioned for the Volkswagen to go by in the passing lane. The Volkswagen did, with a young man driving and the girl beside him wearing a yellow bandana and reflecting sunglasses. She looked at Parker as they went by, and then twisted around to look at him some more through the rear window. "He looked tough."

The young man looked at her, but because of the reflecting sunglasses he saw his own face instead of her eyes. But then she licked her upper lip, the top of her tongue moist and trembling, and he said, "Ah. A ditchdigger."

Parker finished smoking his cigarette, and looked across at Handy. Handy was hunched at the wheel, the position of his body looking nervous. Parker began to wonder if Skimm had been in on the cross. If he had been, she wouldn't be coming along this road. But it didn't make sense that Skimm had been in it, it didn't figure that way at all.

Another car came into sight way down the road and Parker stood up straighter. But when it came closer it turned out to be an old black Packard with a prim old woman at the wheel, and Parker motioned for her to go by in the passing lane. She stopped instead, and leaned out the righthand window. "What seems to be the trouble, young man?"

"Roadwork." he answered.

"It certainly is about time!" She straightened again and drove off.

A little while after the Packard had disappeared at the far curve, Parker saw the Dodge coming. He knew it was the Dodge the second he saw it, and he motioned at Handy. Handy grinned, and let go of the wheel. He could relax now. The Dodge came closer, and Parker could see that Alma was alone in it, so he'd been right all the way down the line.

The Dodge was coming fast, too fast for someone who

couldn't afford to be stopped by the law, and Parker stepped out into the passing lane, and waved the red flag at her, while motioning with his other hand that she should turn right. The car sagged when she hit the brakes, and then she made the turn.

At the last minute, she must have recognized Parker or seen the Ford across the road, because she slammed on the brakes again and tried to get back to the highway, but she was already in too far and her left front fender crumpled into a tree. The Ford came across and turned, blocking the turnoff, and Handy ran over to the Dodge. He had the .38 in his hand, but when he got there the job was finished and Parker was putting the Sauer away again under his shirt. Alma had run only three steps from the car.

They opened the rear door, and Skimm was lying on the money with a paring knife in his chest, which was why she'd taken longer than they'd expected. They pulled him out and got to the money. They stayed behind the Dodge, and the Ford was on the other side of that, so the occasional cars going by didn't bother them.

There were four metal boxes of bills and five bags of coins. Handy took care of the locks on the boxes, and they started to count. The bills were all bound in stacks of a hundred, so the counting didn't take long. There was just over fifty-four thousand dollars in bills.

Parker took out six thousand, for the bankrolling, and they split the rest in half. Parker stowed his share in the suitcase he'd put in the back of the Ford; Handy put his back in two of the metal boxes and stashed them in the trunk of the Dodge. Then Parker picked up a bag of coins in each hand and walked deeper into the woods. The ground was mushy, and when he came to a stream he stopped and dropped the two bags on the ground. On the way back, he passed Handy carrying two more bags in.

Parker went back and got the fifth, and when he got to

the stream again Handy had already slashed one of the bags open and was dumping rolls of quarters out onto the ground, scattering them around. Parker slit open another bag, this one containing rolls of pennies, and walked up the stream a ways, then started dumping. He stamped the rolls of coins into the ground and kicked them into the stream.

It took them a while to get all the coins scattered around. They didn't want them, because they weren't worth the trouble to carry. There was probably less than six hundred dollars in all the five bags put together, and that six hundred was more awkward to carry and more dangerous to dispose of than the entire fifty-four thousand in paper. Banks in the area would be on the alert for a stranger wanting to unload rolls of coins. Getting rid of one roll here and one roll there would be a full-time job. The police knew that, and all professional thieves knew it, and so coins were practically never a part of any boodle.

After they'd finished mining the whole area with rolls of coins, they slashed the canvas bags to ribbons and buried them. Then they went back to the cars. Parker had already moved the detour sign off the road and now he took it deeper into the woods and threw it away. Handy, meanwhile, started the Dodge; hitting the tree hadn't hurt it much, just dented the fender and bumper. It was his getaway car, since he wasn't going back to New Jersey with Parker.

They said so long to each other. "You can get in touch with me through Joe Sheer," Parker said.

"Arnie La Pointe usually knows where I am," Handy answered.

"Right."

Parker turned the Ford around, and headed back for the bridge. In the rearview mirror, he saw the green Dodge come out of the turnoff and go up the road toward the ferry. He took a long way around to get to the farmhouse, not wanting to be too near the diner. He went around through New Brunswick, and it was nearly two o'clock before he got there.

He walked in and the first thing he saw was that the automatic was gone from the card table. The second thing he noticed was that the door to the fruit cellar was still barred. He backed out, looking all around him, and walked around the farmhouse until he came to the ragged hole in the outside wall where Stubbs had knocked the clapboard through and crawled out. He walked over to the dirt road and saw where Stubbs had walked on the soft clay between the tire tracks. He grimaced and went back to the farmhouse and saw that Stubbs had even taken time to shave.

He couldn't wait one more day, thought Parker. He had to go complicate things again. He looked around at the empty slopes around the farmhouse, dotted with scrub. Where the hell have you got to, Stubbs? he thought. Where did you go, Stubbs?

THREE

◆◆◆◆◆◆◆◆◆◆◆◆◆

I.

DARKNESS. Pitch-black darkness, and no sound other than the sounds you make yourself. Blackness and silence and absolute solitude, twenty-two hours a day for two weeks.

Stubbs was lucky. Up and down the country roads of California in the thirties, traveling with the migrant crop-pickers, fighting with the scabs and being stomped every once in a while in a back room by the deputies, had dulled Stubbs' brain. Whole areas of emotion and understanding were muffled for him now, and his brain was no longer capable of complicated thoughts or abstract ideas, and that was lucky. He could stand up under the silent solitary darkness a lot better than a man with a whole brain.

He didn't panic, and he didn't talk to himself, and he didn't concoct crazy complicated schemes that would have forced Parker to kill him. He didn't butt his head against a wall like a rat in a maze. He stopped shaving and he stopped fighting back, because his brain was good enough

93

to tell him there was no reason to shave and no reason to fight back. But other than that he didn't do anything that a more sensitive man might have done.

Since he was starting with only part of a mind anyway, it was easier for Stubbs to revert to the animal. A man with a whole brain would panic first, do all the idiotic things that come from panic, and if he survived the panic then he would be reverted to the animal. For Stubbs it was simpler and more direct.

When an animal is enclosed, he concentrates on only one thing—getting out. And the first way he tries is by digging. Sometime after Parker left on the third day, Stubbs felt his way across the concrete floor to the nearest wall, and then crawled along the wall, feeling the concrete floor and the concrete blocks of the wall where they angled together, looking for a break in one or the other, but he couldn't find a thing. Then he went around again, and this time he found a place where the floor had crumbled a little bit, just at the edge of the wall.

He tried to remember the place without being able to see it, and stumbled away to the broken-down shelves where the farmer's wife had once kept her canning. He got a chunk of wood and went back and for a while he couldn't find the tiny place where the floor had crumbled, but then he did. He poked at the broken place in the floor with the jagged end of the piece of wood, and for a long while he didn't seem to be getting anywhere at all. It would have been easier if he could see what he was doing. Every once in a while he felt the broken place with his fingers, and a few more grains of concrete would brush away, and he'd poke at it some more.

By the time he was too exhausted to work any more he had a hole in the floor the size of his fist. Then he fell asleep, and the next thing he knew Parker was kicking at the door and telling him to come out, and it was the fourth day.

The fourth day and the fifth day and the sixth day he worked on the concrete with chunks of wood, and by the sixth day he had a hole more than a foot in diameter, and he'd started scooping out the dirt. Parker never came into the fruit cellar, because there was no light in there and no reason to go in, so Stubbs didn't try to hide the dirt or the broken rubble of concrete. But on the seventh day he thought to check outside, when Parker let him out, to see just how much digging he had to do.

The land slanted, so that there were only three steps up from the basement level at the back, but around at the side where he'd been working the land slanted up. He judged where the spot would be, and saw that it was impossible. The ground was up the wall on the outside to about shoulder height, judging from inside, and Stubbs knew he'd never be able to get through that. He'd have to dig down first, to get under the wall, and then over, and then up maybe five feet or more. He didn't have any tools, and he didn't have any light, and he wouldn't know whether he was digging in the right direction or not.

After Parker left, that seventh day, Stubbs didn't do anything at all. He sat on the floor in the blackness, listening to his own breathing because that was all there was to listen to, and after a while he felt like crying but he didn't. Even with half a brain, an important failure can affect a man.

The eighth day he stopped shaving, and he stopped looking for an opening when Parker let him out for his two hours in the air. He stopped shaving because he felt despair after the failure of the digging, and he stopped looking for an opening because Parker had never given him one and never would. The ninth day, he didn't do anything.

If an animal can't dig out, it will try to break out, to force his way through the enclosure. The tenth day, after Parker left, Stubbs tried battering down the door. He hit it with his shoulder, and then he backed off and hit it again. That was the closest he came to panic, because of the rhythmic pattern of the movement against the door and because of the pain it made along his arm and shoulder and because the door didn't give at all. When he came close to panic, he stopped hitting the door and stumbled across the black room and sat down.

First the animal tries to go under, and then through, and then over. The eleventh day, Stubbs attacked the ceiling. It was just low enough so Stubbs could strain up on tiptoe and touch the wood between the beams. He knew the farmhouse was sagging and old, and he thought the flooring might be rotten. He got another piece of the shelving and spent a while ramming at the ceiling, trying to break a hole. Because he couldn't see, he sometimes hit the beams instead, and it would jar both arms and sometimes make him drop the piece of wood. Dust and dirt fell down on him as he struck upwards, and he couldn't break through.

Then, on the twelfth day, one of the others gave him a flashlight. At first, he couldn't really believe it, and he kept the joy in, because he was afraid it was a joke or something and they'd take it away again before putting him back in the fruit cellar.

But then he realized it wasn't a joke; Parker was impersonal, not cruel. He never did anything without a reason, and there was no reason to taunt Stubbs, so the flashlight was really his. Parker didn't feel sorry for him because he didn't feel anything for him at all, with the possible exception of irritation. But Handy felt sorry for him, and that was the break.

They put him back in the fruit cellar, and then they left. Stubbs switched on the flashlight and looked at the enclosure. He found the little pile of rubble and dirt where he'd tried to dig his way out, and when he looked for it he saw the scarred place on the ceiling where he'd tried to force his way out. He saw the broken-down shelving he'd been stumbling over from time to time, and he saw his way out.

If he'd had a light before, he'd have been out by now. The wall was concrete block, practically all the way up. But for the last foot, along the outer wall, it wasn't concrete block. The beams rested on the top row of blocks, and between them the wall was just wooden siding, ordinary wooden siding. Stubbs inspected that part of the wall all the way along, and saw how old and rotten and warped the wood looked.

He worked that night, and he worked the thirteenth day except when Parker came to let him out for a while. On the fourteenth day he crawled out onto the ground and rolled over on his back and looked up at the sky. The sun was straight up above him, so it was noon. He lay on his back for a while, smelling the world and looking up at the sky and listening to the small sounds the trees and bushes made in the breeze, and then he got to his feet.

He knew Parker always came in the afternoon some time. He remembered vaguely that Parker and Handy had told him they would let him go soon anyway, but he'd stopped paying attention to what they said. And even if it was just tomorrow when they'd let him out, he didn't want to wait. He wasn't going back in that cellar again.

He went around back and into the basement because he was hungry. He ate cold beans out of a can and drank some water, and then he saw the small mirror Parker had brought with the razor and the can of lather. He looked at himself and knew he had to take a chance on staying long enough to shave.

He shaved, and that made him feel better. Then he took the automatic from the card table and went back around to the side of the house, where he threw out his jacket and cap before climbing out himself. He brushed them off as best he could, brushed his trouser legs, put on the jacket and the cap, and walked out to the road. The automatic was out of sight under his jacket, tucked under his belt.

The first thing he wanted to do was see if the car was still there in Newark. He had money in his pockets, and if the car was still there he could go ahead and do what he'd set out to do two weeks ago, before Parker had trapped him. He didn't want to get even with Parker or blow the whistle on Parker. He wasn't interested in Parker at all, any more than Parker was interested in him. He just wanted to get away and continue looking for the man who'd killed Dr. Adler.

A middle-aged man who said he repaired tractors gave Stubbs a lift into New Brunswick, and from there he took a train to Newark. Once he got to Newark he ran into a problem because he didn't know where the car was. He remembered some street names from when he'd been trailing Parker away from Skimm's house, so he took a cab to one intersection he remembered and walked from there.

It looked different in the daytime and pretty soon he got lost. But then he caught sight of a railroad bridge crossing a street down to his left, and he remembered the car had been left at the end of a street by a railroad embankment.

He picked a direction, hoping it was right, and walked along parallel to the tracks, a block away, looking down each cross street he came to. After a while he saw a church on a corner that he vaguely remembered, so he thought he must be on the right track. He kept going past the church, and two blocks later he saw the car, still parked where he'd left it.

He sighed with relief, because he'd thought the police might have towed it away by now. The engine didn't want to start at first, but after a while it did, and Stubbs carefully turned the Lincoln around in the narrow street.

There were two men left to find, and one of them was supposed to be in New York City. These days he was using the name Wells.

2.

IN 1946, money was loose in the United States. But from another angle, money was tight. That was the year between the war and the cold war, and at the top level money was tight because the men at the top level expected a reduction in government spending now that the war was over. This would mean a reduction in heavy manufacturing and a general tightening of the belt until the nation had made the adjustment from a war to a peace economy. The men at the top gloomily looked forward to a long hard peace, and money with them was tight.

But at the bottom level, money was loose. The servicemen were getting out, and they were getting theirs. The GI Bill let them go to school or buy a house or just sit around on their duffs for fifty-two weeks. The defense plant workers—who'd been getting theirs all along—now had something to spend it on. Cars were being manufactured again and new housing was springing up everywhere, and rationing and other restrictions were disappearing. So the men at the bottom happily looked forward to a long soft peace, and money with them was loose.

There was this man named Wallerbaugh, C. Frederick Wallerbaugh, and he had made a very good living for a number of years by doing the sort of things with stocks that no one is supposed to do. He had a Seat, and his racket was its own respectable front, and no one bothered him. The men at the top ignore the Wallerbaughs for the same reason that a police force retires a graft taker rather than prosecuting him—exposure of dirtiness in a part of the system reflects on the rest of the system. So Wallerbaugh did well, and the only men who could have stopped him ignored him. But in 1946 money at the top was tight, and Wallerbaugh, as usual, had overextended himself.

Wallerbaugh looked around and saw that money at the bottom was loose. He saw what the money was being spent on, and he thought the situation over, and then he became one of the first of the really big-scale Florida land speculators. He had two-color brochures made up, and he sent them out by the bale. There are companies that supply mailing lists of any desired kind—people who own foreign cars; people who belong to correspondence schools; people who have subscriptions to a particular magazine; people who have sent for pornography through the mail—and from one of these Wallerbaugh got a list of ex-servicemen who were married and going to college. Thousands of these got the two-color brochure.

It was a good brochure. It told the ex-serviceman of the unlimited potential of Growing Florida. It told him about the new airplane plants, the industrial boom, the fact that Florida was becoming a First Rate employment market in practically every field. It also told him just how cheaply he could own his own plot of land on Florida's west coast, and how little more it would cost to build a brand new house on that land. The ex-serviceman could start paying for that lot and house right *now,* then it would be ready for him when he graduated from college and he and the Missus were ready for the Big Move.

Wallerbaugh took a lot of servicemen. He sold land that

was totally inaccessible by car. He sold land that was eight feet under water. He sold land to which he didn't hold clear title. He sold land that washed back out into the Gulf of Mexico before the ink was dry on the check.

The Land Grab was bad in Florida for a while, with the speculators all trying to grab from each other, so in 1947 Wallerbaugh took on a partner, a man named Grantz. Grantz had just served a rap for income tax evasion. He'd lived off the black market during the war, which wasn't as easy or as profitable as liquor had once been, and he was happy to bring his know-how into the corporation.

The bubble lasted three years. Wallerbaugh had thought it would last forever, just as the stock game should have lasted forever, but he was wrong. At the top they could afford to ignore him. But now he was working at the bottom, and at the bottom they couldn't afford to ignore him. It was government money, passed by the GI Bill through the hands of servicemen and then into Wallerbaugh's hands, and he was being careless. Grease kept the deal alive for a while, but in 1949 the warrants came out. They arrested Grantz, but Wallerbaugh made it out of the country. His profits were safe in a Swiss bank, and his new home was in Lomas de Zamora, a suburb of Buenos Aires.

But after more than a decade, Wallerbaugh hungered for home again, to be able to move freely in the states once more. Passport and other papers proving him to be Charles F. Wells, retired stockbroker, were expensive to come by but certainly not impossible. But Charles F. Wells had the same face as C. Frederick Wallerbaugh, and that face had been plastered all over the newspapers of the nation in 1949. And for all Wallerbaugh knew that face was still featured on the walls of post offices. The face was a problem; it kept him in Lomas de Zamora a while longer.

Finally he couldn't stand it. Grantz had died of a bad

heart in a Federal prison, but some of Grantz's friends were still around, and Wallerbaugh got in touch with them. A plastic surgeon, somebody good and absolutely trustworthy. The answer came back: Dr. Adler, near Lincoln, Nebraska.

Money made it possible for him to get back into the states, via the Mexican border, without having to test the passport or other papers. Money got him to Nebraska, and more money, to Dr. Adler, got him a new face. After the operation, Charles F. Wells went into Lincoln and bought a new Cadillac and drove it all the way to New York, just for the pure pleasure of being able to look at all that American countryside again.

He had avoided the friends of Grantz, so no one knew that Wallerbaugh was back in the states. The friends of Grantz knew, but they didn't know what he looked like or where he was or what he was calling himself these days. Only one man in the whole world knew enough about Charles F. Wells to be able to call him C. Frederick Wallerbaugh.

After six months, he began to worry. After one month of worry, he decided to act. He had a newer Cadillac by now, and he drove it back to Nebraska. He didn't drive this time for the pleasure, he drove so his name would not appear in the files of any commercial transportation. He drove to Nebraska and shot Dr. Adler and then he drove back to New York. He was safe now, absolutely safe. There was no one left in all the world who could pose any sort of threat to him.

3.

UNTIL he got to the car, Stubbs had thought he would just keep going forward; he would get the car and then go find the man named Wells and find out if he had killed the doctor, and if it hadn't been Wells then he'd go on and find the other man, Courtney. But in any case, all in a straight line, with nothing else in the way. That was because his thinking was muffled and hazy with only one clear spot in the center, able to concentrate on just one train of thought at a time.

But when he got to the car, the impossibility of the straight line forced itself upon his attention. He first began to notice when he had trouble driving the car. His hands seemed thicker and slower on the wheel and one foot was heavy and only partially controlled the accelerator and his other foot was totally out of sympathy with the brake. He kept hitting the brake too hard, and making the hood of the Lincoln dip, and knocking his chest against the steering wheel. And he kept pulling away from traffic lights too fast, nearly stalling the car.

After that, because now he kept looking at his hands, he noticed how filthy they were—covered with small scars and ragged places. And his clothing was a mess. Also his stomach was upset and his nerves seemed bad.

So finally he began to realize that it was impossible, that after two weeks of living like an animal he couldn't just go straight ahead but would have to stop and rest a while. So he stopped. He didn't know about motels, but he knew how to find a hotel in any city. You find the railroad station.

He'd never gone far from the tracks, so he kept on paralleling them, and after a while he found a third-rate hotel. Since it was a third-rate hotel, it didn't have a garage, but the man at the desk told him the car would be safe out in front. Stubbs took his word for it, paid for one night, and got his two suitcases from the trunk.

There was no shower in his private bath, but there was a tub. He sat for an hour in water nearly too hot to stand, adding more hot water every time the water in the tub started to cool. After that he went directly to bed, though it wasn't even seven o'clock yet.

He woke at eight-thirty the next morning, and his head was buzzing. His nerves were far worse than yesterday, so bad that his arms and legs were shaking. He lay on his back on the bed, and his forehead was burning up. He felt a dull anger at the symptoms, because they were keeping him from the straight line, and he tried to ignore them. He pushed the covers away and got out of bed, but he immediately became dizzy and fell, hitting his face on the floor.

After a while, he got to the telephone and told the man at the desk that he needed a doctor. The man at the desk was irritated, and showed it, but he did send a doctor. He was a paunchy man with gray hair and a no-nonsense scowl, and when he came in, using the key the desk man had given him, Stubbs was back in bed, not wholly conscious.

The doctor examined him, and asked him questions he had a difficult time answering. Then he closed his black bag with a snap. "You have to stop drinking. You know that, don't you?"

"I haven't been drinking," Stubbs told him. "I never drink." It was true. Alcohol, even when he was at his best, hurt his head.

The doctor frowned, not sure whether or not to believe

him. It being this particular hotel, this particular *kind* of hotel, the doctor had been prepared to diagnose even before seeing Stubbs. He stood looking down at him, and now he saw that the symptoms were not exactly right. Some of the symptoms that should have been there weren't, like a craving for water and a special soreness in the joints of the arms. "Then you've been working too hard. Some sort of heavy physical labor without proper nutrition. You haven't been getting enough sleep or enough rest or enough of the right kinds of food. Am I right?"

It was close enough. Stubbs nodded.

The doctor nodded, too, satisfied. "I don't suppose you want to go to a clinic?"

"No."

"I thought not. Can you pay for a nurse? You need someone to bring you food, at least for a day or two. You can't leave that bed."

"In my wallet," Stubbs said. He motioned at his pants folded on the chair. "Take some for yourself and a nurse."

The doctor was surprised at how much money there was in the wallet, and it made him curious as to what this man had been doing to get so run-down and have so much money, but he kept his curiosity to himself. He was a doctor with a small practice in a poor neighborhood, plus work at a clinic, plus being house doctor for this hotel and two others very much like it. He had the constant feeling that violence and evil were all around him, kept just out of sight because these people needed him as a doctor, but if he were ever to turn his head fast and see the evil they would have to kill him, whether they needed him or not. Because of this, he had trained his curiosity to be a small and private thing.

He took some money from Stubbs' wallet, showed him how much he had taken, and explained what each dollar of it was for. "The man downstairs said you'd only paid for one night. I think you'll be here four more days at the very least."

"Pay him for two," said Stubbs.

The doctor argued with him, but Stubbs ignored him. He concentrated on the straight line and lay quiet in the bed so he'd be well sooner, and after a while the doctor stopped arguing. He shrugged, and took some more money from Stubbs' wallet, and left.

The nurse was bitter Irish, thin-bodied and sharp-faced, and a rosary rustled in her starched pocket. She fed him, when her watch said it was time and not when he was hungry, and she took good care of him without ever talking to him. It embarrassed him to use the bedpan, but she insisted. She came for two days, because that was how much she'd been paid for. The second day he didn't really need her, but she came anyway and wouldn't let him out of the bed. He decided to get up as soon as she left, but he didn't.

The third day he was on his own again. He got up and stood beside the bed, and he wasn't dizzy. He felt weak, and very hungry, but that was all, and the trembling in his arms and legs had stopped. He got clean clothing from his suitcase and went out to a restaurant for breakfast.

He walked around a little afterwards, but then the dizziness started to come back, so he went back to the room and lay down on the bed and slept some more. When he woke up it was afternoon, and he went out again for another meal. On the way out the desk clerk stopped him, and he paid for another day.

The fourth day, Friday, he was himself again. He'd nearly forgotten the two weeks at the farmhouse. It was only a dim memory, soft with lost details. In the clear spot in the middle of his brain, the straight line was back.

He packed the two suitcases, stowed the automatic under his coat, and went out to the car. Charles F. Wells lived somewhere in New York.

4.

Stubbs closed the phone book and put away his ball-point pen and the old piece of envelope and walked back out of the drugstore onto 10th Avenue. He stood blinking in the sunshine, not knowing where to go next, where to start. Then he thought of maps, so he went back into the drugstore. "Do you have a map of New York?"

"Manhattan?"

Stubbs frowned. "New York," he said again, because he didn't know what else to say.

Manhattan, decided the druggist. He reached behind him and got a small red book. The book was full of the locations of streets and information about subways and places of interest, and pasted in the back of the book was a street map of Manhattan.

Stubbs paid his quarter and took the little red book and started out of the store. Then he stopped again, struck by a sudden suspicion, and went back. "What about the rest?"

The druggist just looked at him. "The rest?"

Stubbs concentrated, and came up with a name. "Brooklyn."

He was remembering now that New York was in parts. Manhattan was one part, and Brooklyn another. And there were other parts.

"Oh. You want a map of Brooklyn, too?" The druggist started to reach behind him again.

"No," Stubbs pointed toward the phone booth. "About the phone book," he said. "Is it just Manhattan?"

"Of course."

"You don't have the others?"

The druggist shook his head. "Why don't you try Grand Central. They've got books from all the boroughs of Greater New York and the suburbs there."

Stubbs nodded. "Grand Central," he repeated. "Where's Grand Central?"

The druggist opened his mouth, then hesitated. "Look, let me show you. Give me that map."

Stubbs handed over the little red book. The druggist opened the map in the back, and showed him. He was here, 10th Avenue and 39th Street. Grand Central was over here, 42nd Street, the other side of 5th Avenue.

Stubbs nodded. "Thank you."

"Not at all." The druggist folded the map up for him and handed him back the little book. Stubbs went out to the sidewalk.

In his mind, it had seemed simple. He would come to New York and look in the phone book and it would say Charles Wells and give an address, and he would go to that address. So when he came through the Lincoln Tunnel he parked as soon as he saw a drugstore, and he looked in the phone book. There was a "Wells, C." and a "Wells, C. F." and two "Wells, Charles", Four people in New York that might be the man he wanted.

And then at the last minute he'd been reminded that New York had other parts, like Brooklyn. Charles F. Wells might not be any one of these four, he might be somebody else entirely, in Brooklyn or one of the other parts.

He stood on the sidewalk, and he didn't know what to do next. He could go look up the four people he already had, or he could go to Grand Central and maybe make the list longer. He thought about it and decided it would be better to try these four people first, and only go to Grand Central if none of the four was the man he wanted. But then he was afraid he wouldn't be able to find Grand Central once he'd left this spot, this spot was the only place he knew how to find Grand Central from. So while he still remembered where it was, he got down on his knees on the sidewalk and opened the map up and made a mark with his ballpoint pen where the druggist had said he could find Grand Central. A woman going by looked at him in surprise and then, seeing the map, she smiled.

After he made the mark, Stubbs got to his feet again, put the pen away, folded up the map, and walked back to where he'd parked the car. He sat in it and took out his list of four names, and with the help of the book he found out where each of them lived.

C. Wells lived on Grove Street. That was downtown, in a section called Greenwich Village, which was not separate like Brooklyn but was really a part of Manhattan. It bothered Stubbs that the city had parts, and even the parts had parts. He put the map away and started the car.

He went the wrong way at first, but then he asked directions of a cop giving out parking tickets, and after that he went the right way. When he got to Greenwich Village he had to stop at the curb almost every block and look at the map, but finally he found Grove Street, and even a parking space.

The building he wanted had a narrow foyer with mailboxes and doorbells, and next to one of the doorbells was the name C. Wells. It was kind of a rundown house for a man as rich as Charles F. Wells had seemed, but you never knew if a rich appearance was just front. Stubbs rang the bell, and a buzzer sounded, releasing the door lock.

It was a walk-up. A door was open on the second floor, and a sharp-featured girl in her twenties was standing in the doorway. She had long black hair hanging straight down her back, and she was wearing a flannel shirt and dungarees. Her face looked dirty the way a face looks when you eat too much fried foods. She watched Stubbs coming up the stairs.

Stubbs came up to the top step. "I'm looking for C. Wells."

"I'm C. Wells," she said.

"The C. Wells in the phone book?"

"What is this?" she asked. Her voice and face were both getting sharper.

Stubbs persisted. "Are you the C. Wells in the phone book?"

"Yes, I am," she said, "and what the hell business is it of yours?"

"All right." He turned around and started back down the stairs.

She came to the head of the stairs, frowning, and looked down. "What the hell do you want, anyway?"

"Nothing," he said, not looking back. "It isn't nothing."

"Hey, just a goddam second!"

Stubbs went on down the stairs.

"I'm calling the cops!" she shouted, and stormed back into her apartment.

Stubbs went out to the street and back to the car, and looked at his list and the map again. C. F. Wells lived on West 73rd Street, and when he looked at the map he saw that that was a long way uptown. He sighed and started the car. Once he got above 14th Street, the going was easy, because all the streets were numbered, and as long as the numbers kept getting higher he knew he was going the right way.

It was another apartment house, but a better one, bigger and cleaner and not converted from a brownstone dwelling. But it still wasn't any place where a rich man would live. Stubbs pressed the button beside the name C. F. Wells, and when the buzzer sounded he went into a quiet foyer with a rug. There was an elevator, self-service, and he rode it up to the fourth floor and then knocked on the door of apartment 4-A.

A young man in khaki pants and an undershirt opened

the door, and stood there scratching his head. Stubbs had obviously waked him up. "I'm looking for C. F. Wells," Stubbs said.

"Clara? She's at work."

"That's the C. F. Wells that's in the phone book?"

"Yeah, it's in her name, that's right." The young man stopped scratching, and yawned. "You from the phone company?"

"No," said Stubbs. "I'm looking for a person."

He turned away and went back to the elevator. The young man stood in the doorway, scratching himself here and there, and frowned at the disappearing Stubbs, but he didn't say anything. Stubbs got into the elevator and went downstairs and back to the car. Both of them were women, so far. Why didn't they put their whole names in the book?

He looked at his list. One Charles Wells lived on Central Park West, and the other Charles Wells lived on Fort Washington Avenue. Central Park West was closer, and sounded rich, so he tried that first.

There was a doorman at this building, but he didn't stop Stubbs or ask him any questions. Stubbs got the apartment number from the mailbox and took the elevator up.

A middle-aged woman answered his knock. She looked severe, and when Stubbs asked her if Charles Wells was home she said, "My husband is at work."

Stubbs thought about that for a minute, while the woman asked him if he was applying for the chauffeur's job. "Does this Charles Wells have black hair except gray around the ears and real thick eyebrows?"

The woman looked surprised. "My husband is bald."

"Been bald long?" Stubbs asked.

"For years. What in the world is this all about?"

"I'm looking for a Charles Wells. But he isn't the right one."

Fort Washington Avenue was way uptown, up by the

George Washington Bridge. Stubbs found a parking space on 181st Street and walked back to the address. It was a walk-up again, and Charles Wells lived on the third floor.

When Stubbs knocked, the door was opened by a young man in his early twenties. He wore tight black slacks and an orange shirt with the tails tied in a knot over his ribcage, leaving his midriff bare. His eyes were made up and he had rouge on his cheeks. His hair was far too long, waved, and dyed a rich auburn. He struck a pose in the doorway. "Well, look at *you!*"

"I'm looking for Charles Wells," Stubbs said.

"Well, you just come right *in,* dearie."

"Are you Charles Wells?"

The boy made a kissing motion. "Come on in, dearie, and we'll talk about it."

Stubbs frowned. He remembered this kind of boy, there'd been some in the Party. Not many, but some, and Stubbs had never liked them, because he'd thought they'd give the Party a bad name. Not that it mattered in the long run. But he also remembered that there was only one way to get this flighty type to calm down and make sense, so he reached out and thumped the boy gently on the nose.

The boy's eyes started to water, and his face squinched up, and he made a sound like a mouse when the trap hits it, only smaller.

"Are you Charles Wells?"

"My nose," said the boy.

Stubbs held up his fist. "Yes or no."

"Yes! Yes! Don't you *dare—*"

"All right," Stubbs said.

He went back downstairs. Four possibilities, and none of them had been the man he wanted, and two and one half of them had been women. He went back to the car and drove to Grand Central Station.

It was impossible to park anywhere around that area, since it was now five-thirty Friday afternoon and the middle of the week's worst rush hour. Stubbs pushed the Lincoln around in the traffic for a while until he saw a sign that said, "Park." He turned in at the garage entrance, and got out of the car. A man came up and asked him how long he'd be and Stubbs said just a little while. When the attendant took the car away, Stubbs walked back to Grand Central.

There was a whole rack of phone books, alphabetical and classified. There was Manhattan and Brooklyn and Queens and the Bronx and Nassau County and some other suburbs. Stubbs got out his old envelope and ballpoint pen. He ignored the suburbs and just looked in the books for Brooklyn, Queens, and the Bronx.

If Charles F. Wells was in New York, he was in New York and not someplace nearby.

When he was done with the three phone books, Stubbs had eleven more possibilities.

5.

It took all of Saturday and most of Sunday for Stubbs to find out that none of these eleven was the right Charles F. Wells either. He had found a hotel on the west side of Manhattan that looked close enough to the one in Newark to be its twin, and when he got back to his room from the Bronx late Sunday afternoon he didn't know what he was going to do next. He sat on the bed, because there wasn't any chair, and smoked cigarette after cigarette and tried to think.

Charles F. Wells lived in New York. But he wasn't in any of the New York phone books. Did that mean he wasn't in New York after all? Or merely that he didn't have a telephone? Or that he had an unlisted number?

If he lived in New York that was supposed to mean that he lived in New York. So the thing to do was to figure that he either had no phone at all or a phone with an unlisted number. And since he was a rich man, then he had a phone with an unlisted number.

Stubbs put out his cigarette and immediately started a new one. All right. This Wells, the one Stubbs wanted, had an unlisted telephone number. That meant Stubbs couldn't find him in the phone book, which meant that Stubbs would have to find him some other way.

Thinking, struggling for an answer, Stubbs remembered the old days when sometimes a situation like this would come up. You'd go into a city and there was a man you were looking for and you had to find; he was with you or against you or you needed him one way or another. But then there had been the Party, and the local contacts. Always the local contacts, either Party people or sympathizers, and you could go to them and tell the problem to them. They knew the local situation, they had an in here or an in there, and they could find your man for you. But now there wasn't any Party any more. And anyway this situation didn't have anything to do with the Party.

Stubbs rubbed his head and remembered the days in the Party, the good times when thoughts slid through his head like they were on wheels, when he knew the questions and the answers. He didn't know now what he thought of the Party, whether he thought what had happened to him had been worth it or not, because he never really thought of the Party at all but only of people. He remembered faces from that time, and frozen moments of import in strikes, like the moment when the deputy had driven his car over the little girl. That had been good because it had solidified the workers and made the strike as hard as steel, until some damn fool had killed a foreman over a personal grudge, and then predictably the workers had become afraid and the strike had fizzled out.

It was strange, in a way, that now it was only the people he remembered. At the time he had never thought about people at all, but only of issues, of theories and dogmas and the masses, and now that it was all over and half his brain had been lost in the fight he never thought of the issues at all.

Charles F. Wells. He brought himself back from remembering, angry at himself for losing the straight line again even for just a minute. He had to find Charles F. Wells. Not with the Party, because that was a dead thing now, but by himself.

Except he didn't know what to do next.

Wells was in New York, that much he knew. How did he know it? Because May told him. How did May know it? Because Wells had talked with her and with the doctor and with the two nurses, and Wells had said that after the bandages came off he was going to go live in New York.

Buy a house in New York.

Stubbs squinted up his face, and stared at the pattern on the bedspread. Was that what May had said? Charles F. Wells was going to go live in New York, go there and buy a house, and he already had a couple of real estate agents looking around for him. That's what Charles F. Wells had said, and that's what May had told Stubbs, and Stubbs had forgotten all of it except the part about New York.

The two weeks in the darkness at the farmhouse had made him forget a lot of things, and this important thing about buying a house was one that he'd forgotten. He thought now of the apartments he'd been to, apartment buildings all over New York, and all that time wasted. One of the people he'd gone to in Brooklyn had lived in a house, and two of the people in Queens, but none of them had lived in the kind of house a rich man would live in. Where in New York would there be the kind of house a rich man would buy ánd live in?

Then he thought of the suburbs. If a rich man was going to buy a house somewhere right near New York, would he say he was going to New York to buy a house? Yes, he would. And if a man wanted to be handy to New York but also wanted privacy the way Charles F. Wells wanted privacy, would he most likely try to live outside the city limits? Yes, he would.

Stubbs was relieved. He'd thought it out by himself, he'd made his brain go to work after all and remember important things and make important decisions. He put out his latest cigarette and got off the bed, smiling, and left the hotel and walked across town to Grand Central again.

There was a phone book for Nassau County, and the map in the front of the phone book showed that Nassau County was on Long Island, just beyond Brooklyn and Queens. And in the W section there was a listing for "Wells, Chas. F." Stubbs knew it was the man. He knew without a doubt that this time he'd found the right man. He copied the address and phone number down, and closed the phone·book.

Walking across the terminal, he looked ahead and saw Parker. He stopped in his tracks, not believing it, and then other people got in the way and he wasn't really sure it had been Parker he'd seen. Maybe his brain was playing tricks on him. Nevertheless, he turned around and went off in another direction.

6.

At Huntington, twenty miles from the city line, Stubbs stopped and asked directions again. He asked in a bar, because there'd be more people there to work out the right answer among them, and they all cooperated, the way he'd expected, contradicting each other and suggesting alternate routes and finally hammering out a course for him to follow. He thanked them and finished the beer he'd bought just as a token, and went back out to the car.

He followed the directions.

He stayed on 25A through Huntington and out the other side and kept going till he saw the Huntington Crescent Golf Course. After that, he made the left where they'd told him, and two turns later he was on Reardon Road, near the Sound, though he couldn't see any water. He stayed on Reardon Road, a winding blacktop road with trees surrounding it on either side and occasional breaks where a narrower winding blacktop road went off to one side or the other. At each break he slowed down, till at last he saw what he wanted. There was a rural delivery mailbox on a wooden post by the road, with stone gateposts behind it and the usual narrow winding blacktop road going in among the trees. This time on the mailbox it said, "Charles F. Wells."

Stubbs turned the Lincoln slowly and drove through the stone gateposts. He leaned forward over the steering wheel and reached out and removed the automatic from the glove compartment. He put in on the seat, where he could reach it fast.

The blacktop road was barely two car-widths, and it

wandered and curved back and forth amid the trees. They were thin-trunked trees, young, with the branches starting high up and with not too much underbrush between them. Stubbs rolled along in the Lincoln at a bare ten miles an hour, peering ahead around the curves to see the house, and when he saw it he hit the brake and stopped.

It was stone, and old. Stubbs could just barely see it ahead and to the right, through the tree trunks. He backed up just a little, till the house was out of sight, and then he turned the engine off. There was no place to pull off the road, so he just left the car where it was and climbed out.

It was nearly evening, seven-thirty or so, and the spaces between the trees were getting dimmer. Stubbs moved away from the car and the road, going in among the trees, moving at an angle toward the house. Soon he could see it again, and then he crouched and moved more slowly.

The house was big, two stories high and rambling. There was a screen-enclosed wooden porch around the first floor and the rest was stone. To the right of the house, the blacktop road ended at a three-car garage, stone like the house and with white doors.

A slate walk joined a small side door in the garage and the side of the house, with an arched roof over the walk, supported by rough unpainted wooden posts. The garage had a second story, with windows in it, but they were dark, without curtains or shades. In the house, two windows on the ground floor showed light, and so did one window upstairs.

Stubbs crept forward toward the house until he came to the edge of the trees, where the blacktop widened in front of the house before coming to a stop at the garage. He could try to cross the bare blacktopped area here, or he could go to the right through the trees and around the garage, to come at the house from the back. That would probably be better.

He remembered how easily Parker and the other one had turned the tables on him, and he didn't want it to happen again. If Wells wasn't the one and it was Courtney, it wouldn't be too bad; but if Wells was the one and he turned the tables on Stubbs it would be the end.

He made his decision, and started to the right. He'd taken two steps when a voice behind him said, "That's far enough."

He stopped. In that second, he cursed himself, cursed the brain that had gone rotten and prevented him from doing what he had to do, that made him such a feeble hunter and such easy prey.

"Drop the gun," said the voice, "and turn slowly around."

There was nothing else to do. He hoped it was Courtney, and that Wells was in the clear. He dropped the gun and turned around, and saw Wells standing at the edge of the blacktop. The man had been in among the trees even before Stubbs had got there, and had followed him when he left the car. It was still getting darker, but not dark enough to prevent a good shot, and in the hand not holding the gun Wells carried a flashlight.

Wells looked at him, frowning, and then smiled. "The chauffeur," he said. "I'd forgotten about you."

Stubbs licked his lips, wanting to ask the question but afraid it had already been answered.

"You shouldn't have phoned," Wells went on. "That put me on my guard, you know."

Stubbs shook his head, and was about to say he hadn't phoned, but just then Wells shot him. Something heavy, feeling much larger than a bullet, hit him in the chest, knocking him backwards. His mouth was still open. He still wanted to tell Wells that a mistake had been made, that he hadn't phoned, but he couldn't manage to exhale. No air came out, he couldn't make a sound.

He felt himself falling. It was getting darker much more

rapidly all of a sudden. Then he saw Wells' face, and Wells was looking past him, at something behind him. There was on Wells face an expression of astonishment and terror. Stubbs, falling forward toward the blacktop and the spreading blackness, wondered dully why Wells looked so astonished and so terrified.

But he never found out.

FOUR

◆◆◆◆◆◆◆◆◆◆◆◆

I.

PARKER got back into the Ford, and drove away from the farmhouse. He turned the car toward New Brunswick, northwestward. First things first.

Stubbs was gone. Parker had to find him again before he got himself killed and gave the cook back in Nebraska a reason to blow the whistle, but first things came first. Riding in the Ford with Parker was thirty thousand dollars in green paper, and until he'd found a safe place for that boodle he couldn't afford to do anything else.

He had to follow the plan, with or without Stubbs.

But as he drove along he was nagged by a feeling of incompletion. There was a spiel worked out in his head that he'd been planning to give to Stubbs: "You come with me on this one side trip. It'll take a couple of days. Then we take a plane to Nebraska and square things with the cook, and after that I'll give you some help finding the man you want."

The last part was the only lie, but it was a necessary lie because it would give Stubbs a reason for going along with no fuss. The whole spiel was good and simple and direct, and it would have gone down with no trouble at all.

Except that Stubbs was gone, and the spiel would never be delivered. He didn't like sloppiness, loose ends that unraveled, complications of things that ought to be simple. Stubbs was a complication in what should have been a simple job, and now he was complicating the complication. So Parker did what he always tried to do—keep it simple, keep close to the plan, don't let yourself get knocked off balance.

First things first. The boodle had to be unloaded, that came first. The cook in Nebraska would wait two more weeks before blowing the whistle, and it might take Stubbs a while to find the other two men he was looking for. So first things first.

At New Brunswick, he picked up route 1, and that took him southward again. The afternoon sun lowered to his right. At Trenton he switched to 206, and got on the Jersey Turnpike at Mansfield Square. He hadn't seen a single roadblock, and that made sense. The robbery was more than three hours old when he'd left the farmhouse, and the law would have to figure that the thieves were either out of the area by then or holed up somewhere in it. Parker had used the principle of the delayed getaway before, but never quite this way—getting out of the area fast and then going back into the area and coming out again.

He took the most direct route south, sometimes on 1 and sometimes on quicker roads. He bypassed Washington the same way as when he'd come north with the truck, and when he passed through Richmond it was ten o'clock at night. He stopped in a motel on the other side of town, and brought both his suitcases into the room, the one with his clothes and the one with the money.

He picked a stack of twenties, all used bills, stuffed fifty of them back into the suitcase with the rest of the money and the other fifty into his wallet. The wallet was so thick then it didn't want to fold. Then he went to the motel office and got a cardboard box and some string and wrapping paper.

Eleven thousand went into the box, which he then wrapped up and addressed: Charles Willis, c/o Pacifica Beach Hotel, Sausalito, California, Please Hold. Unless the Pacifica Beach had changed hands in the three years since he'd last been there, they would know enough to stick the carton into the hotel safe and forget about it till Parker showed up again.

There was stationery and envelopes in the drawer of the writing desk in the room, and Parker addressed five envelopes to Joe Sheer in Omaha and put ten twenties in each envelope, wrapped in sheets of blank stationery. Joe wasn't a drop and it wasn't any kind of a debt, just a friendly gesture.

There was still sixteen thousand in the suitcase. In the old days, before Lynn and the syndicate trouble had loused things up, he'd had small bank accounts here and there across the country. After a job he'd send off a lot of hundred dollar money orders from different towns, and spread a few thousand of the take that way. Then when he needed money all he had to do was withdraw a little· from here and a little from there, and avoid the kind of unexplained large bank transaction that might call attention to itself. But Lynn had closed out all those accounts when she'd thought she'd killed him and had run off with Mal. So now he had to start all over again.

After he was finished distributing the money, he locked up the suitcase and went to bed. He fell asleep right away, but within half an hour he was awake again, and he wasn't sure why. He lay on his side, trying to go back to sleep, and finally he rolled over onto his back and smoked a cigarette and stared at the ceiling, wondering why he couldn't sleep.

And when he thought about it, it was simple. Another change from the years when he'd had Lynn. During the planning of a job, the build-up and the waiting, he'd never been any good with a woman, not even Lynn. But as soon as the job was done and turned out right he was always as randy as a stallion with the stud fee paid. After the jobs, before this, there'd always been Lynn, and before Lynn there had always been *someone*. This time there wasn't anyone at all.

He finished his cigarette, and then he gave up and got out of bed. He dressed in the dark, took all but a hundred dollars from his wallet, and stuffed the other nine hundred under the mattress. Then he went out to the Ford and drove back north to Richmond.

He didn't know Richmond very well, only having been through the town once or twice before, but finding a woman was never hard in any town big enough. You just go where the neon is mostly red.

2.

IN the morning he left her and went back to the motel. He picked up his gear and headed south again. He stopped in Petersburg and opened a checking account in the Petersburg & Central Trust Co., with an initial deposit of four hundred dollars. A bank in Raleigh got three hundred sixty and a bank in Sanford four seventy. After that it was too late in the day, the banks were all closed.

He crossed into South Carolina that night and stopped at a motel just north of Columbia. He locked the money in the trunk of the car, so he could bring the whore from Columbia back to the motel. He sent her to the motel lunch counter alone for breakfast in the morning while he got some more cash from the car. Then he drove her back to town and stopped off to deposit four hundred twenty dollars in a Columbia bank.

Augusta got three fifty, and for the rest of the day the towns were too small to take a chance. He crossed into Florida at nine-thirty and got just south of Callahan before picking his motel for the night. Jacksonville was twenty miles away, so that's where he went for a whore. She was the same as the Richmond whore and the Columbia whore, disinterested till he hurt her a little. He didn't get his kicks from hurting whores, it was just the only way he knew to get them interested.

Thursday morning he put four hundred forty dollars into a bank in Jacksonville, and Thursday afternoon he deposited three hundred eighty more in a bank in Daytona Beach.

The stopping at banks and the late starts because of the whores were slowing him down, so he didn't make Miami Thursday night the way he'd planned. Around midnight he stopped at Fort Pierce, a hundred and thirty miles north of the city. He slept alone that night, having rid himself of most of the urgency. He could now wait for something decent in Miami, something that wouldn't have to be slapped before she'd get interested.

A Fort Pierce bank got three hundred ten the next morning, and around noon he stopped at West Palm Beach, off the Sunshine State Parkway, long enough to leave three hundred and seventy more. Then he got back onto the Parkway, with thirteen thousand five hundred still in the suitcase.

He hit Miami in mid-afternoon, got back onto route 1, went south past Coral Gables, and stopped at the Via Paradise Hotel, a huge lumbering white sand castle that looked like a pueblo rebuilt by Frank Lloyd Wright. The doorman who helped him out of the car and the bellboy who ran to get the two suitcases both looked dubious, because he was rumpled and mean-looking from the trip. But both had been working there long enough to know you couldn't tell a guest by the way he looked when he showed up.

Parker gave the doorman a half and asked him to take care of his car. Then he went inside, following the bellboy. This was a resort hotel, which meant too many bellboys, so they had to work the guests' luggage in a sort of relay race. Parker was ready with another half dollar when the bellboy abandoned his suitcases at the desk.

Tourists tip quarters and spenders tip dollar bills and people who live in resort hotels as a way of life tip half dollars. Now both the doorman and the bellboy knew that the rumpled clothing and the unprepossessing Ford could be discounted.

The desk clerk caught the tone in the bellboy's "Thank you, sir," and came over smiling. "You have a reservation?"

"Yes, I have." Parker's voice was softer now, his expression more civil. He wasn't working now. "The name is Willis. I wasn't expected till Monday, but there was a change in plans. I hope it isn't inconvenient?"

"Not at all, not at all." The desk clerk went away, and came back with an outsize card. "Is that Charles Willis?"

"That's right."

"No trouble at all, Mr. Willis."

A couple of months from now, when it got colder up north, it would be a lot of trouble, but not now.

"Is Edelman around?" Parker asked.

"Yes, sir, I believe he is. His office is—"

"I know where it is."

"Yes, sir."

The desk clerk got him signed in and told him his room number, and bellboy number two appeared. Parker gave him a half dollar and the suitcase with the clothes in it. "Take this up to my room, will you? I'll hold onto the other one."

"Yes, sir."

The bellboy went away, carrying the suitcase, and Parker went around the corner and down the hall to the door marked, "Samuel Edelman, Manager" on the frosted glass. He went inside and the secretary stopped typing and looked at him.

"Charles Willis to see Mr. Edelman."

"One moment, please." The girl went inside to the inner office, and Parker waited, holding his suitcase. After a minute she came out. "Mr. Edelman will see you."

"Thank you." Parker went inside, and she closed the door after him.

Edelman was standing up behind his desk, a stocky thin-haired man who gave the impression of being tightly girdled. He looked the same as ever, but Parker didn't, because of the new face, and that's why Edelman looked anxious and indignant. "I thought you were a different Charles Willis. One I used to know."

"I am." Parker put the suitcase down and smiled, waving a hand in front of his face. "Plastic surgery. I know, my wife told you I was dead."

"She was quite certain of it," Edelman said. He sounded oddly prim, as though he suspected some sort of blasphemy.

"Lynn, you mean. She had to act that way." Parker sat down in the brown leather chair in front of the desk. "I ran into a little trouble and had to change things around a little. "Charles Willis" is a common name, and I still have a lot of friends I don't want to lose track of, like you, so I kept it. But I had to be out of sight, so I had to get a new face."

Edelman remained standing, but doubt furrowed his brow. "She took the two packages, you know."

Parker nodded. He knew she'd cleaned out all the caches. "Of course she did," he said. "But now everything's all right again. I've got the new face, and everything is straightened out."

Edelman's eyes narrowed, showing he was thinking. "Is Mrs. Willis with you?"

"Unfortunately, no. We had a tense time there for a while, and she didn't like having to play-act, tell everybody I was dead and so forth. It got on her nerves, and we quarreled a lot, and—" He shrugged. "—we parted."

"There's some similarity," Edelman said, studying Parker's face, "but I don't like it. First Mrs. Willis tells me her husband is dead, and then you come in and say you're Mr. Willis and your wife has left you. I don't like it."

"You must have my signature around on something." Parker reached out and took the gold pen out of the ornate pen holder. There was a memo pad on the desk, and he wrote the name "Charles Willis" on it five times. "Go ahead and check it."

"You could have practiced the signature."

Parker shrugged. "Ask me something. Let me make like that Princess Anastasia for a while. Ask me something only Willis would know."

Edelman closed his eyes. "The voice sounds right." He opened his eyes again. "You understand, it's a surprise. I'm not sure what to believe."

"People get into trouble." Parker shrugged. "I was in trouble for a while, that's all. If someone had come around looking for me, you could have told them you'd heard from my wife that I was dead. If someone comes around now and wants to know am I the same Charles Willis who used to come here, you can say no—that Charles Willis is dead, this is another one."

Edelman at last sat down behind the desk. "All right. What problem did you help me solve seven years ago?"

"Cantore, the bookie that wanted to open an office in the hotel. He had somebody working in the kitchen, lousing up the food with Tabasco sauce, and you asked me to talk to Cantore. I did, and the problem went away."

Edelman nodded. "You could have heard that from Willis."

It was time to show impatience. Parker said, "Damn it, man, I *am* Willis. I know you can't stand your middle name, which is Moisha. I know you like to be called Sam and hate to be called Ed or Eddy. I know you drink nothing but wine, but you'll drink any kind of wine that can be poured. I know you've got a boat called the *Paradise* and I was on it when you caught a marlin one time, and I was on it when you let marlins get away half a dozen times. All right now?"

Edelman slowly smiled. "Like Mark Twain, the reports of your death are greatly exaggerated. But at least Twain came back with his own face."

Parker shrugged. It was time for a light remark, but he had trouble thinking of light remarks. "You satisfied now?"

"Yes, I suppose I am."

"Fine."

Now that the matter was settled, Edelman could be the hotel manager again. "You'll be staying with us for a while?"

"A couple of months at least. But I'm going to have to be away for a few days. I'm just settling in for now." He kicked the suitcase. "I want to leave this in your safe."

"Of course. Wait, I'll give you the receipt for it."

They talked a while longer, so Edelman could get used to the fact that Parker was still alive, and then Parker went up to his room. He had a view of the beach, with the bright umbrellas and the bright beach mattresses and the people in their bright bathing suits. He unpacked the suitcase and loafed around the room a while, unbending, and then went downstairs to the hotel men's shop.

He bought a bathing suit, and some clothing, and had them sent up to his room. Then he went around to the garage and got the Ford. He drove out south on route 1 to Homestead, and then took 27 in toward the Everglades. At a deserted spot he turned right onto a dirt road and followed that deep into the swampy area, and then stopped the car.

He searched it carefully, under the seats, on the floor, for anything that might lead to him, then did the same in the trunk. When he was satisfied it was clean, he took the license plates off. Jersey plates could lead to trouble. He carried them away into the swamp and buried them.

He left the key in the ignition. Now someone else could have the Ford, and if the law ever got interested in it Parker would be too far back in the chain of events to be traced.

And Charles Willis didn't own a car.

He walked back to 27 and hitched a ride to Homestead. From there he took a cab back to the hotel.

3.

THE car rental agency was as good as its advertising. Parker got off the plane in Lincoln at three-thirty on Saturday morning and the Chevrolet was there waiting for him. He signed the papers, showed the driver's license he'd bought in New Jersey, and drove off.

He was in a hurry, but it was too late at night. He was in a hurry because it was now nearly a week since Stubbs had escaped from the farmhouse, but it was too late at night because he was tired and he wasn't sure what sort of reception he'd get at the sanatarium. Stubbs had said something about the cook having her common-law husband with her. So Parker drove the rented Chevvy into town where he got a hotel room and slept till ten o'clock. He had a hurried breakfast and then drove out to the sanitarium.

It had only been three weeks since the death of Dr. Adler, but already the place looked as though it had been abandoned for years. Parker drove up past the neglected lawns to the front door and stopped the Chevvy where the sign marked "Visitor's Parking."

This was going to be a delicate situation, and the best thing would be to come in openly, as though there was nothing to hide.

He got out of the car and walked up to the front door, which opened just before he got to it. A broad-shouldered heavy-browed man in corduroy pants and a flannel shirt stood in the doorway glowering at him. "What you want?"

"I want to talk to—" He couldn't remember the cook's name. "—I want to talk to the cook."

"You mean May?"

"That's it."

"Hold it a second." But he didn't go anywhere, just stood in the doorway staring distrustfully at Parker. "What you want to talk to her about?"

"About Stubbs," Parker said, "and why I didn't kill him."

He frowned massively at that, and took a step back from the doorway, but held onto the door. "Who are you supposed to be?"

Parker said, "Let me talk to May."

From deeper inside the building, a woman's voice called, "Who is it, Lennie?"

Lennie turned to shout, "Hold on a goddam minute!" Then he looked at Parker again. "What's the name?"

"Let me talk to May. She'll recognize me."

But then May was at the door, staring out at him. "That's one of them!" she shouted. "That's Anson, the last one!"

"He said something about Stubbs."

"Don't let him get away!" May shouted.

"Yuh." Lennie came out across the threshold, his arms reaching out, and Parker hit him under the ribs. He made a dull sound and bent forward, and Parker said over his shoulder, "Tell him to back up."

But May was ignoring him. She was turned away from the door, screaming, "Hey, Blue! Hey, Blue!"

Lennie was getting his wind back. In a minute, he'd try again, and maybe by then he'd have Blue to help him. Parker didn't like the way it was starting out, but the thing to do now was to simplify the situation as much as possible, and the first way to simplify it would be to remove Lennie. So Parker chopped him in the Adam's apple and clipped him on the temple, and then kneed his face as he was going down. And then Blue came through the door.

Blue was a yapping terrier of a man, short and wiry and ferocious, with a sandy moustache to match his sandy hair. He came in holding his arms like a man who'd taken a correspondence course in judo, so Parker stuck out his right hand for Blue to play games with. And while Blue was grabbing the arm and getting set for an over-the-shoulder toss Parker hit him with a left to the kidney and a left to the ear and a knee to the groin. Blue folded, letting go of Parker's arm, and Parker used the right on his jaw.

Blue and Lennie were both out now and Parker looked around to see May racing down the hall deeper into the building. Knowing she was headed for a gun, Parker took off after her. He caught her just as she was going into Dr. Adler's office. He grabbed her shoulder, spun her around, and slapped her openhanded across the face. The slap shocked her, but it was the spin that threw her off balance. She sat down on the floor, heavily, and Parker stood over her and showed her his fists. "Do you listen, or do I beat your head in?"

"Blue!" she wailed.

"They're out of it. Both of them."

But May wouldn't give up. She came off the floor trying to kick him in the groin, and he grabbed her ankle and dumped her again. Then he knelt on her chest and slapped her till she stopped waving her arms around. "Now," he said. "You ready to listen now?"

"Get off me."

She sounded calm, so he got off her. She sat up, slowly, as if checking for broken bones. "When Blue wakes up," she said, "he'll murder you."

"If he tries, I'll put him to sleep again."

She looked up at him then, and finally it seemed to dawn on her that he could do exactly what he said. She rubbed her chest where he'd knelt on her. "What do you want here, anyway?"

"Tell Blue and Lennie to leave us alone while we talk."

She thought it over, and then nodded.

He helped her to her feet, and she walked back down the hall toward the front door. Parker stood by the doctor's office, watching her. When she got to the entranceway, Blue and Lennie were both getting up, unsteadily. She talked to them, and they glared at him past her shoulder. After a while, they both nodded reluctantly, and then all three came back down the hall.

"You talk to all of us," May said.

Parker shrugged. He turned his back and walked into the doctor's office. He hitched one buttock onto the corner of the desk and looked at them, all three of them standing just inside the doorway. "You want to sit down?"

"Get to it," May said. She was the spokesman for the trio, and the brains.

"All right. Stubbs braced me about three weeks ago, with an elephant gun."

Lennie interrupted. "Where'd he get one of those?"

"The automatic," Parker said patiently. "I took it away from him and heard his story. I had proof I was in New Jersey the Saturday the doctor was killed. Stubbs heard me out, and he was satisfied. But then he wanted to go after the other two. He said there was three he was looking for."

The woman nodded. The other two just watched.

"I didn't let him go. Stubbs is willing, but he's stupid. He braced me and a friend of mine, and we took the gun away from him with no trouble. If he went up against the guy who killed your doctor, he's dead."

"That's up to Stubbs," said May.

Parker shook his head. "It's up to me. Stubbs told me you were set to blow the whistle on three people if he didn't get back in time. So the killer gets Stubbs, and then you people get me."

"Don't you worry about Stubbs," May said. "He's good with his fists, and he's good with a gun."

"But he's bad with his mind. That's the part that bothers me."

"It's probably all over now anyway," she said. "He's had three weeks."

Parker shook his head. "I put him on ice for two weeks. I was going to bring him back here, let him clear me with you. But he got away Monday, just before I was done with the job I was on."

"Wait a second," said May. "Back up there a second. Are you telling me you kidnapped Stubbs?"

"I put him on ice. There was a job I was on, and I couldn't spare the time away from it, so I was keeping him till the job was over. But he got away a day early."

"Why, you son of a bitch," May said. "You stand there as cool as you damn please and tell me the way you treated Stubbs?"

Parker shrugged, irritated. That part was over, there was no need to harp on it. "I've got a new face to protect. I didn't kill your doctor, and I've got no stake in finding the guy who did. There was no reason to let you and Stubbs louse up a job I was working on."

Lennie said, softly, "Blue and I could take him, May, if we was to come at him together."

"No," May said. "He hasn't got to what he wants yet."

She was brighter than Stubbs anyway. Parker said to her, "I want to know who he's going after now. Number two and number three. I want to catch up with him before he gets himself killed, and bring him back here so I'm in the clear."

"Are you out of your mind?" She put her hands on her hips and leaned toward him, her face outraged. "Are you stark staring crazy? You say you proved to Stubbs you didn't kill Dr. Adler, let's see you prove it to me."

"I can't, without Stubbs."

"Why not? How'd you prove it to him?"

Parker shook his head. It was taking too long, and not getting anywhere. "I was in a diner that Saturday," he said. "I had Stubbs check with a waitress who knew me there."

"So I'll call her now. Long distance."

"She's dead."

May nodded, as though he'd just proved a point for her. "That's real convenient, isn't it?"

"I want to know where Stubbs is," Parker said. "The reason I gave you is the truth. What other reason would make sense?"

"Maybe you want to catch up with him and kill him because he knows you really did kill Dr. Adler."

"Then why would he be still going after the other two?"

May's face was closed, she'd made up her mind. "I wouldn't know about that."

Parker tried one last time. "If I wanted to kill him, why didn't I do it when I had my hands on him?"

"Maybe you never did," said Blue. His voice was yappish, like a terrier's.

"You're as stupid as Stubbs. How would I know about you people here if I hadn't talked to Stubbs?"

"The hell with you, mister," May said. "We don't tell you anything. When Stubbs comes back, he can tell us about you himself."

"And if he doesn't come back?"

"We let the outfit know about your new face."

There was no sense talking any more. Parker looked at Lennie and Blue, trying to decide which was the common-law husband, and picked Blue, the one with the moustache. He took the Sauer out from under his jacket and shot Blue in the left elbow. It was a quick loud clap of sound in the room, and Blue screamed and sat down on the floor. His face drained white, and his right hand came over, shaking, to touch his shattered elbow.

Parker looked at May. "The next one I give him is in the knee. That's even tougher to fix. He'll never walk right again as long as he lives."

May and Lennie were both staring at the gun, their faces as white as Blue's. May's mouth opened, but no sound came out.

Parker felt the heft of the gun in his hand. "The simplest way," he said thoughtfully, talking more to himself than to them, "would be to kill the three of you. Then Stubbs gets himself killed, and from then on everything is roses."

"Wait," May said, her voice an octave higher than before.

"It would be simplest."

"Number two is named Wells," said May, talking so fast the words tripped all over each other. "His real name is Wallerbaugh, but he's calling himself Wells. And number three is named Courtney."

Parker lowered the gun. There wasn't enough reason to kill these three. It was dangerous to kill when there wasn't enough reason, because after a while killing became the solution to everything, and when you got to thinking that way you were only one step from the chair. Parker had killed without enough reason twice, both times because he was impatient, and one time the killing could be matched to an FBI card with his prints on it. He wasn't going to make any more mistakes like that.

"All right," he said. "You give me the details. And then you wait out the month, just like you planned. If neither Stubbs nor I come back by then you can do whatever you want. That's only a week from now."

"All right," May said. "All right. All right."

4.

PARKER took the Carey bus from La Guardia to the East Side Terminal building on 37th Street in Manhattan. A rented Chevrolet was waiting for him there, but he let it wait a little longer, while he went up to Grand Central. It was five o'clock Sunday afternoon, and the station was doing a thriving business. Parker worked his way through it to the phone booths and the telephone books.

Buying a house had meant suburb to Parker from the beginning. The East Side Airlines Terminal had the phone books for the boroughs of New York—except for Staten Island—but the man Parker was looking for would be in Nassau County or Westchester County, or maybe even in Fairfield County up in Connecticut.

There was a "Wells, Chas. F.," in Nassau County. Parker knew from May that Stubbs had planned to go through the phone book for all the possibilities and then go visit each one. He also knew that Stubbs would start with the city itself.

But sooner or later it would have to occur to Stubbs that Wells lived outside the city, and Stubbs was six days ahead of him. There wasn't time to do it the way Stubbs was doing. Parker looked at the phone number for this Nassau County Wells, got some change out of his pocket and went into one of the booths.

He talked with an operator first, and fed some more money into the slots. Then the ringing sounded in his ear. He was just about to give up, after ten rings, when the phone was answered by a male voice. Parker said, "I want to talk to Charles F. Wells."

"Speaking."

"This is Wallerbaugh."

If he was the wrong Wells, he'd be baffled. If he was the right Wells, the name coming at him this way might throw him off base.

It did. There was a pause, and then the voice, wary and careful. "What was that name, please?"

"Dr. Adler," Parker said. Just to be absolutely sure.

The wait was longer this time, and the voice this time was low and vicious. "Who are you? What do you want?"

Parker hung up. He left the booth and went back across the crowded terminal floor and took a cab back to the Airlines Terminal. It was the right Wells, and he was still alive. That could mean Stubbs hadn't found him yet, even though he'd had six days. Or it could mean Stubbs had found him and Wells had proved his innocence. It could also mean that Stubbs had found him and was now dead.

The address wasn't much to go on. Reardon Road, Huntington, Long Island. There was a map in the glove compartment of the rented Chevrolet, and Parker found Huntington and figured out his best route. The Queens Midtown Tunnel, because it was handy to the Terminal, and then the Long Island Expressway. Glen Cove Road up to North Hempstead Turnpike, which was also 25A, and that road into Huntington. When he got there, he could ask directions to Reardon Road.

He put the map back in the glove compartment.

5.

PARKER walked into the bar and ordered a beer. Outside, evening was coming on, and this was the first bar he had come to in Huntington. All of the normal bar bric-a-brac was on display—the Pabst Blue Ribbon antique car; Miss Rheingold; the Budweiser hanging clock; the Miller's High Life dancing lights; the light shaped like a 7; the Schlitz clock against a pattern of spangled blue. Half a dozen locals sat along the length of the bar, and three more were playing the bowling machine in the back. One of them was a lefty.

Parker drank half the beer. "I'm looking for Reardon Road."

The bartender looked at him and said, "You, too?" Then he turned to somebody else sitting at the bar. "Here's another guy looking for Reardon Road."

"Is that right?"

"You mean my brother's been here already?"

"Your brother?"

"Older than me. Short and stocky and looks maybe a little punchy."

"Well I'll be damned," said the bartender.

The local the bartender had talked to came over to Parker. "He was in here maybe half an hour ago."

"Less than that," said the bartender.

Parker drained the rest of the beer. "I thought I was ahead of him. Which way did you say it was?"

"Reardon Road?" The customer looked at the bartender. "How did we tell his brother to go?"

Another customer came down the line. "I was the one

told him. Look, Mac, you go straight on through town on this street, see? And then you keep on going straight till you see the golf course."

"The Crescent," said the first customer.

"Right. The Huntington Crescent. And you make a left just the other side of the golf course."

"First left," said the bartender.

"Right," said the second customer again; he didn't like to be interrupted. "And then you make the second right and the first left."

The other customer and the bartender nodded. "That's the way we told him."

Parker repeated it back. "First left after the golf course, then second right and first left."

They all told him that was right, and he thanked them. Then he went back out to the car and drove through town, staying within the speed limit all the way. This was no time to waste fifteen minutes arguing with a cop.

The golf course was farther from town than he'd expected, but maybe that was because he was in such a hurry. Stubbs was less than half 'an hour ahead of him. But because of the phone call, Wells was forewarned.

Distances are deceiving on narrow blacktop country roads. The second right was forever after the first left, and the next left was across the rim of the world in Asia someplace. Then at last he was on Reardon Road, and he had to crawl to be sure of reading the names on the mailboxes. He spotted Wells' name at last, and pulled the Chevvy off the road. He couldn't see the black Lincoln parked anywhere, so Stubbs must have just blundered on in, driving the car.

Parker got out of the Chevvy, locked it, and walked down the private road among the trees. He came around a turn and there was the Lincoln, parked, blocking the road. He took the Sauer out and moved up slowly, but the car was empty. He went beyond it, saw the house, and cut away to the right into the woods.

If Stubbs had any sense, he was working his way around through the woods to the back of the house. Or he'd done it already. There were lights on in the house and Parker caught occasional glimpses of them through the trees. He kept bearing right, until he knew he was beyond the house, and then he angled to the left around it.

All of a sudden there was blacktop in front of him, and he was looking at the three-car garage. He cursed under his breath and took a backward step, and then he heard the shot to his left. He rushed out to the blacktop and looked down to the left and saw Stubbs there, in the evening gloom, folding forward into himself. Beyond Stubbs was another man, distinguished-looking and white-haired, holding a gun. Wells looked past Stubbs and saw Parker, and his eyes widened as the gun came up, ready for another shot.

Don't kill him yet, Parker told himself, *and don't ruin his right hand.* He fired low, and the bullet shattered Wells' ankle. Wells made a strange high-pitched "Aaahh," and pitched forward onto the blacktop. The gun skittered away and stopped next to Stubbs' ear.

Parker checked Stubbs first, and he was dead. Then he checked Wells, who was unconscious. He ripped the sleeve from Wells' shirt and made a hasty tourniquet around Wells' leg to keep all the blood from pumping out through the ankle. Then, holding the Sauer again, he trotted across the blacktop and into the house.

It was a fine old house; the original owners had probably been Tories.

Parker went from room to room, switching on the lights, leaving them on in his wake. The light gleamed on polished mahogany and brass, on rich flooring and rich woodwork, on muted oil paintings and shelves of books.

In the kitchen, the light was fluorescent, and shone on

porcelain and stainless steel and formica. Parker went upstairs and prowled all the rooms, and then went down into the basement, where he found the servants' quarters. But there was no one in the house.

Finally he went back outside, leaving the house ablaze with light. Outside it was fully night. Parker looked at the windows on the second story of the garage, but they were uncurtained except for a film of dust. He went across the blacktop to where the two men were lying, and found Wells crawling toward Stubbs and the gun.

Parker kicked him on the bad ankle, and he fainted again. Then Parker picked him up and carried him into the house and dropped him on the leather sofa in the living room. He'd never seen a leather sofa before; it must have cost around a thousand.

When Wells came to again, Parker was sitting in a chair near the sofa, the Sauer held easy in his lap. Wells blinked in the light, and whispered, "My leg. My leg."

"I know you killed Stubbs. Did you kill Dr. Adler, too?"

"My leg," Wells whispered.

Parker grimaced. He'd have to start with an easier question. "Where are the servants?"

Wells closed his eyes. "I need a doctor."

"Answers first."

"I gave them the evening off."

Parker nodded. "So there'd be no witnesses when you killed Stubbs? You killed Dr. Adler, too?"

"My leg. I need a doctor, I can't stand the pain."

"Answers first. You killed Dr. Adler?"

"Yes! Yes, you knew that already."

"I wanted to hear it." Parker got to his feet and walked out of the room.

Behind him, Wells cried, "For the love of God, I need a doctor!"

Parker remembered a study. He found it and searched through the desk drawers till he found pen and paper. On the way back he passed through the music room and took down an LP in its jacket to write on.

Wells was still on the sofa, his eyes closed. When Parker came in he opened them. "Did you call a doctor?"

"Not yet."

"The pain, man."

"That's nothing." Parker lifted Wells to a sitting position, the bad leg straight out in front of him, heel on the floor. Then he loosened the tourniquet. "Watch the ankle."

Wells watched, and saw the blood suddenly spurt. It had practically stopped before, and started to coagulate, but when the tourniquet was released the clot broke down. Wells groaned, and reached for the tourniquet.

Parker slapped his hand away. "You've got something to write first." He gave Wells the LP and the paper and the pen. "Write how you killed Dr. Adler and Stubbs."

"I'm too weak! I'm losing blood!"

"You could die," Parker said, "if you waste time arguing."

Wells' hands were shaking, but he managed to write: "I leaned in the window from the porch, and shot Dr. Adler as he was sitting at his desk. I fired four times. I waited in the woods for—"

He paused and looked up. "What was the chauffeur's name?"

"Stubbs. With two b's."

"—Stubbs and shot him when he came into the open in front of my house."

Parker read over his shoulder. "Sign it."

"Charles F. Wells."

"The other name, too."

"C. Frederick Wallerbaugh."

"Fine."

Parker took the confession away so no blood would get on it, and then fired the Sauer once. The bullet caught Wells in the heart.

Parker put the Sauer away under his jacket and waved the confession in the air till the ink dried. Then he folded it up and put it in his pocket, and went out to the kitchen to find a knife.

6.

IT took him only three days to drive to Lincoln, because he was on turnpikes most of the way. They'd given him a Pontiac instead of a Chevrolet for the one-way rental from New York to Lincoln, and it was just old enough to be broken in, so he made good time. He took only one side trip, to pick up the typewriter case full of money from the motel outside Pittsburgh.

It was just eleven o'clock Thursday morning when he drove up to the sanitarium building. In the four days since he'd seen it, the further deterioration in the place was visible. It was falling apart fast, in the hands of May and her two men, and they'd probably abandon it before winter.

As Parker got out of the car, carrying the overnight bag, Lennie and Blue came out onto the porch and stood looking at him. Blue's left arm was in a sling, and his color wasn't good. They both seemed surprised to see him.

Parker came up onto the porch. "Where's May?"

Lennie blinked. "We didn't expect to see you no more."

Blue said, "Where's Stubbs?" His yapping voice was weaker than before, but still belligerent.

"May first," Parker said.

"Here I am."

Parker looked past the two men and saw May in the

semidarkness just inside the doorway. She was glaring at him, and holding an old Colt Peacemaker in both hands, her right hand holding the grip and the trigger and her left hand holding the barrel.

"You'll burn your hand off, you shoot that gun when you're holding it that way. And break a wrist while you're at it."

"Don't you worry none about me," she said. "What are you doing back here?"

"I said I'd be back."

"Where's Stubbs?"

"He's dead."

"You killed him."

"Wells killed him." He walked toward her, between the two men, and the gun wavered in her hands. She seemed to be debating in her mind. When he was almost upon her, she lowered the gun, sullenly, and let it hang heavy and ineffectual from her right hand.

"Come on," he said. He walked around her and led the way down the hall to the doctor's office. He could hear them whispering behind him, Lennie or Blue whispering urgently to May, and May making sounds of anger.

In the office, he set the overnight bag down on the floor beside the desk, and turned around. The three of them were standing the same as the other time, just inside the door—May in front, Blue behind and to her right, Lennie behind and to her left. They looked like bowling pins.

"All right," May said. "I suppose you still got that funny-looking gun. But this time I've got one too, and don't let my skinniness fool you. You make one funny move and I'll shoot you before you can blink an eye."

"I'm sure of it. I'm going to get a piece of paper out of my pocket."

"Move slow," May warned him.

Parker reached into his inside jacket pocket, and came

out with the folded confession. He walked across the room and handed it to May.

She didn't know what to do with the Peacemaker. She couldn't unfold the paper while she was still holding it. Finally, reluctantly, she handed it over to Blue. "Keep your eye on him."

"Don't you worry about that," Blue said.

May read the confession and Blue and Lennie read it over her shoulder, Blue forgetting all about watching Parker. Parker could have walked over and taken the Peacemaker away from Blue, but there was no point in it. He leaned against the desk and waited.

May finished first, because the other two were lip-readers. She looked over at Parker. "How do I know this isn't a phony?"

"Is that his real name there, down on the bottom? C. Frederick Wallerbaugh?"

"So what?"

"All you told me was 'Wallerbaugh.' Not the first and middle names, or how he signed himself."

"That's right, May," Lennie said. It was a surprise to hear him talk. Parker looked at him and tried to decide if Lennie was still wearing the same undershirt he'd had on last Saturday. The corduroy pants were the same.

"All right," said May. She wanted to be difficult, and there was always a way. "How come he wrote this?"

"I'd shot him, and he wanted me to get him a doctor."

"You forced him. So maybe it's a pack of lies."

"What for?" Like the last time, Parker was having trouble keeping hold of his temper. But he didn't want to get too impatient, because then he'd kill these three morons, and that would be their brand of stupidity.

"So we'd think it wasn't you killed Dr. Adler and Stubbs."

"Why did I kill Dr. Adler and Stubbs?"

"So they wouldn't tell nobody about your new face."

"Then why didn't I kill you three the last time I was here?"

"That's right, May," Lennie said. Parker looked at him, surprised again. Maybe Lennie was the one with a mind in his head.

"All he's trying to do is fast-talk us again," May said.

"But why would he kill the doctor and Stubbs, and then not try to kill us? Why should he try to fast-talk us?" Lennie asked.

May shook her head, truculently. "I just don't trust this man."

"I don't think I should trust you either," Parker said. "I trusted the doctor because he had a brain, and because a friend of mine vouched for him. But you three are morons."

"Hold on there." The Peacemaker had been dangling from the end of Blue's arm, but now he managed to bring the barrel up and aim it at Parker.

"Now, wait, Blue," Lennie said. "If this man's trying to be fair to us, we ought to try to be fair to him." His face was screwed up with concentration, the way Stubbs had done sometimes when he was thinking hard. "You got to admit he makes sense. All he's been doing is trying to prove to us he didn't kill the doctor, when it would have been easier for him to kill the three of us. If he'd killed the doctor that's just exactly what he would have done. And besides, May, you said he wouldn't come back and that would prove he was the killer. But he did come back after all."

May thought that one over, not liking it because it cleared Parker and she didn't like Parker. Finally she shrugged, reluctantly. "I suppose that's right."

But Parker wanted to be sure. "Wells killed your doctor. You got that straight now?"

"I suppose so," May said. She was frowning hard now, and she looked at Lennie as though for help.

"We got to be fair with this man, May. He went to a lot of trouble to prove himself."

May shook her head. "You better give me that gun back, Blue."

Parker studied them, frowning, and then grimaced in disgust. "You already blew the whistle!"

May had the gun again, holding it in her two-handed grip, aiming it shakily at him. "Now, you stay right there."

"You couldn't wait," Parker said. "You had to be damn fools."

It was Lennie who answered, apologetically. "We figured you for a phony," he said. "We got to talking it over, and May thought—we all thought you were just out to kill Stubbs, that you'd sold us a bill of goods. May said—we all figured you wouldn't be coming back. So I went down into town, and talked with a guy I know. He works for the bookie's wire service, and he made a couple phone calls, and then I talked to another man on the telephone—"

"Who?"

"I don't know, named Lowry, something like that. And I gave him your description."

"You acted so goddam *tough*," May cried.

"Not tough enough. I should have burned you, all three of you. I should have known I couldn't trust you."

Lennie, still apologizing, said, "It wouldn't of been fair not to tell you. After all the trouble you went through. We did wrong, but it wouldn't of been fair not to tell you."

Parker considered. The thing was shot now. The syndicate didn't have a picture of him, and a description always fits thousands of men, but they did know about the new face. They knew now not to look for Parker the way he used to be. He felt like taking the Peacemaker away from May and using it on the three of them, but it wouldn't do any good.

So what now? He could go find himself another plastic surgeon, run the whole thing again, but the hell with it.

You could never be sure, never be absolutely sure. Doing it this way, running away and trying to hide from the syndicate, that had been wrong from the beginning. He had his own life to live, his own pattern, his own plans and pace. What good was it to change all that? He might just as well let the syndicate kill him.

What he had to do was make sure the syndicate was convinced they should forget him. He had to make them hurt, he had to bring them down to where they'd be willing to throw in the towel. Then he could go on about his business without worrying about new names or new faces or new days of life.

The three of them were watching him, warily. Finally Lennie said, "What do you figure to do now?"

"With you people? Forget you."

"We're sorry, Mr. Anson," Lennie said. "Honest to God."

There was no sense talking to them. They were idiots, but they'd done all the damage they could do. Parker started through them, out of the room, but Blue said, "You forgot your bag."

Parker paused and looked back at the overnight bag. "Oh, yeah." He went back to it. "Stubbs told me one time, if anybody tried to kill the doctor to protect their new face, Stubbs would take the new face away from them. Stubbs got killed, so I did it for him."

He picked up the overnight bag and set it on the desk. There was a zipper around three sides, and Parker unzipped it all the way around. The flap fell open, and May and the two men looked at the new face Dr. Adler had given to Charles F. Wells.

They were still staring at the head when Parker walked through them and down the hall and out to the car. He paused beside the car to light a cigarette, then climbed in behind the wheel and drove back out to the road. He'd give the car back to the rental people. And after that—?

After that, Miami. The syndicate trouble had to be settled, but it could wait. Parker had to unwind for a while, for a few weeks anyway. It would be good to be Charles Willis again for a time.

The Gregg Press Mystery Fiction Series
Otto Penzler, *Editor*

The Case of the Baker Street Irregulars by Anthony Boucher
A Gentle Murderer by Dorothy Salisbury Davis
One More Unfortunate by Edgar Lustgarten
The Dark Tunnel by Ross Macdonald
Green Ice by Raoul Whitfield
Manhattan Love Song by Cornell Woolrich

Hard Cain by James M. Cain
You Play the Black and the Red Comes Up by Richard Hallas
Headed for a Hearse by Jonathan Latimer
Six Deadly Dames by Frederick Nebel

The Early Philo Vance by S.S. Van Dine

The Benson Murder Case
The "Canary" Murder Case
The Greene Murder Case
The Bishop Murder Case
The Scarab Murder Case
The Kennel Murder Case

Boston Blackie by Jack Boyle
Fog of Doubt by Christianna Brand
The Fabulous Clipjoint by Fredric Brown
The Three Coffins by John Dickson Carr
The Floating Admiral
by Certain Members of the Detection Club
The Eighth Circle by Stanley Ellin
Before the Fact by Francis Iles
The Moving Target by Ross Macdonald
The Dead Letter by Seeley Regester
Rendezvous in Black by Cornell Woolrich

The Great Merlini:
The Complete Stories of the Magician Detective
by Clayton Rawson
Death From a Top Hat by Clayton Rawson
The Footprints on the Ceiling by Clayton Rawson
The Headless Lady by Clayton Rawson
No Coffin for the Corpse by Clayton Rawson

COLOPHON

This Gregg Press edition is designed to last
more than a lifetime. It is printed on paper free
of acids that normally yellow paper, sewn in
signatures so that the pages will not
easily fall out, and bound to
library standards in
sturdy and durable
buckram cloth.